MW01168665

ZINA PATEL

Wish You Had Told Me

First published by Zina Patel 2024

Copyright © 2024 by Zina Patel

All rights reserved. No part of this publication may be reproduced, stored or transmitted in any form or by any means, electronic, mechanical, photocopying, recording, scanning, or otherwise without written permission from the publisher. It is illegal to copy this book, post it to a website, or distribute it by any other means without permission.

This novel is entirely a work of fiction. The names, characters and incidents portrayed in it are the work of the author's imagination. Any resemblance to actual persons, living or dead, events or localities is entirely coincidental.

Designations used by companies to distinguish their products are often claimed as trademarks. All brand names and product names used in this book and on its cover are trade names, service marks, trademarks and registered trademarks of their respective owners. The publishers and the book are not associated with any product or vendor mentioned in this book. None of the companies referenced within the book have endorsed the book.

First edition

ISBN: 979-8-9897500-0-9

This book was professionally typeset on Reedsy.
Find out more at reedsy.com

Destined to be friends, for a reason, a season or a lifetime.
Grateful for every friend.
If we've lost touch that doesn't mean you've left my heart.

A sweet friendship refreshes the soul.
— Proverbs 27:9

"Friendship is the hardest thing in the world to explain. It's not something you learn in school. But if you haven't learned the meaning of friendship, then you really haven't learned anything."

— Mohammad Ali

"Do the best you can until you know better. Then when you know better, do better."
— Maya Angelou

Wish You Had Told Me

Zina Patel

1

Chapter One: Life Comes At You Fast

The paramedic flashed me a perfect smile that could rival any toothpaste commercial, and his voice, deep, and velvety smooth, was like a DJ soothing the beats of my chaotic heart, which according to my Apple Watch was doing its best impression of a racehorse at the Kentucky Derby. Modern technology, a blessing and a curse.

Following the emergency call guidelines, I sprawled out on my foyer's slate floor like a drama queen in distress, awaiting the LAFD squad. In no time, my place was swarming with uniformed heroes armed with sticky sensors and a portable EKG machine. My private panic party had been quickly crashed, thank God, and for a moment, I reveled in the reassurance that I wouldn't be dying alone.

Only a few minutes passed since I hit the panic button on the ADT panel, and there they were, which is a miracle in itself with LA traffic. I expected to be loaded onto a stretcher, a one-way trip to the hospital, but nope. All clear. Normal. Just another panic attack. Again.

Breathless, unsteady and sweaty, but so grateful that nothing was physically wrong, I gathered myself together and propped up against the wall.

The paramedic leaned in, flashing that warm smile that felt like a hug seasoned with chicken noodle soup and a side of hot cocoa. "Maybe you should see someone, get some therapy, and you'll be fine."

Fine. He was fine. Fine AF. Maybe he was onto something; therapy could be my next hot date.

The panic attacks were playing hide-and-seek with my sanity, and the constant 4 a.m. anxiety was not only annoying, but also seriously messing with my beauty sleep. Was I hustling too hard, or not hard enough? It was like trying to find the perfect balance between a kale smoothie and a double-shot espresso.

Once the paramedic packed up his gear, leaving me in the aftermath of my personal soap opera, I was left alone in my echoey, oversized stone foyer. My interior designer was right, I definitely should have used warmer materials. I remember it clearly, do you want the first impression of your home to be cold and hard? And I remember thinking, well, I want stone because I want this house to last through the storms of life. Build your house on rock, its Biblical. Well, we were both right, I have the stone, it is sturdy but, wow, is it frosty. Might be time for a re-design? That can be solved on another day, but for now, I need to get some sleep, or at least try.

4:44 a.m.

Wide awake again, heart racing. Hot and sticky. Its not even summer yet, but I'm roasting under this down comforter. Insomnia had become my annoying bedfellow, denying me the rest I craved. For the past couple of hours, I've been tossing and turning like a wannabe gymnast, caught in a circus act of bizarre dreams.

It's official—I'm a certified insomniac, and this nocturnal nonsense has gotten way out of hand. I rolled onto my back, and gazed up at the ceiling fan, performing its lazy ballet routine in slow motion. It was as if it was saying, 'Hey Ava, watch me spin and cool you down, while you contemplate the mysteries of life at the crack of dawn.' Thanks, fan, but I was hoping for a hard-bodied hubby in my king-sized bed by now. Instead, it's just me, flying solo. My dreams of a busy, happy home filled with rambunctious toddlers, crumbs everywhere, laughter and a lovable chaos have been long deferred. But hopefully not denied.

Years ago now, turning thirty had been a wake up call in so many ways, and not all good. Who would have thought that so much could change in just a few short years. Certainly I'm grateful for my business success, but at what cost? For the past ten years, I've kept my head down and worked hard, and still made time to be part of society, volunteering and cheering on other people's success- celebrating my friends' milestone moments, with generous gifts and sincere enthusiasm. I 'liked' all the social media posts, first day of school pictures, graduation pics, and every birthday that appeared on my news feed. I'd hopelessly stared at engagement announcements, wedding and anniversary photos, and wondered how it seems everyone else is holding it all together. (Meanwhile, over here, panic attacks are on the regular menu.)

Instagram moments of the journey of others, encapsulated in carefully cultivated and filtered snapshots, left me wondering if I was the only one feeling like my own life was a bit of a jigsaw puzzle, missing a few crucial pieces. I really felt, deep down, like I *almost* had it all figured out, but something was for sure missing. Therapy? Would that be the key?

The very milestones I celebrated for others only seemed to highlight the void in my own story, leaving me wondering if I had unknowingly become the supporting character in the grand narrative of my own life. I knew deep in my soul that I needed to embrace my 'main character energy' and make some serious changes.

So much had already changed, beyond my control, which was frustrating.

Three of my closest friends, who I assumed would be my lifetime besties, had gone their separate ways. Vanished into thin air as if the memories and moments we'd shared meant nothing. If I'm being honest, I played a role in how we fell out. *A small role.* But a role, nonetheless. We'd all gotten to a place where we were growing in different directions. I was ambitious, chasing my career goals and starting my own media company; Lauren disappeared into marriage and motherhood; Camille, well that's a whole different situation; and Olivia, she was being her usual self-centered self.

All of those components thrown into a bucket had left us on opposite sides of the fence, and even on opposite coasts now. In our twenties, we developed different responsibilities, formed new bonds, discovered separate interests and outlooks on what friendship looked like as young adults. It was times like this when I remembered what my mother used to say all the time. *"Ava, you won't have the same friends at thirty that you have in high school or college."* I always hated when she said that because it sounded harsh, callous even, and I didn't see it that way. I never saw my friendships as anything other than lifetime bonds.

Boy was I wrong.

Betrayal, jealousy, and life wedged themselves between us. The timing just never seemed to work out that we were all happy at the same time. At the time we parted, I was so engrossed in building my company, I didn't stop to really assess what really caused us to fall apart. Since no one else did either, I focused on becoming the best in my business, and before I knew it, their absences became a distant thought. Perhaps, now that I was older, I could see how that wasn't the best way to go. Putting forth some effort to keep in touch through the years, anything even close to the same effort I gave my business, would've been a better option. Not doing that is why I was alone with no one to share my success with. On my big milestone birthday, at that, and it stung.

I turned my head to see a sliver of sunlight peeking through my blackout curtains that I hadn't closed all the way. I rested my cheek on the silk pillowcase that promised to prevent wrinkles, to stare at the tiny crack of daylight. I could see the orange and yellow layers hovering above the trees as the horizon began to push the dark hues of blue further up into the clouds. A new day was dawning and I was determined to make some necessary changes.

I closed my eyelids briefly before the four minutes of rest I had were up. My alarm clock started to sound, and I rolled back over to silence it. I didn't have to be up this early since my office didn't open until nine, but I cherished the peace and quiet, and appreciated this time to gather my thoughts before heading out.

Normally I worked out and did a brief meditation with yoga stretches, but I wasn't in the mood today. My head wasn't in the right space to focus on a workout this morning. Lately, especially this morning for some reason, all I thought about was how I was soon about to enter into another decade, still as single as a missing sock left in the dryer.

And on top of all of that, I had absolutely no idea what I wanted to do to celebrate my birthday. My cousin, Jade, had been bugging me nonstop about what my plans were. Each time I thought I had a plan, I arrived right back where I started— nowhere. I considered doing a small family thing, but quickly vetoed that idea. Spending my birthday listening to my aunties remind me of how I should already be married with kids— all of my cousins, plus my younger sister and brother were doing their part in continuing the Richards line, and if I didn't put a move on it, my eggs would shrivel up — was not the celebratory vibe I cared to subject anyone to, including myself.

As if I needed a reminder.

I swung my legs over the side of the bed and slid my feet inside the soft, shearling slippers I brought back from Harrods on my last trip to London. They were the perfect wintertime slippers, if only Los Angeles actually had real winters. We had occasional chilly nights, but nothing compared to the intensely cold evenings I recalled from my childhood on the east coast. Sometimes I missed winter and the simple pleasures of the season: embers crackling in the fireplace, that delicious wood-burning scent, snuggling under cozy fur throws in pajamas, drinking hot cocoa that warmed my entire body, while staring at a blanket of fluffy snow that covered the grounds outside of our window.

Wintertime on the east coast was beautiful. Picturesque. Serene. It always motivated me to slow down and appreciate the change of seasons. In LA, aside from the slight shift in temperature, I rarely saw any difference in seasons. Every day was just "another day in paradise." But also, every day time was ticking by and you might not even notice, thanks to the steady seventy two degrees temperature and perpetual sunny weather.

I stretched my arms and pushed myself off the bed. Picking up the remote, I turned on CNN to get the daily dose of disappointment. I was never a fan of the news when I was younger. It always seemed like a drag to watch. However, with everything going on these days, I'd be doing myself a disservice by not watching. If the pandemic year had taught us anything, it was the importance of staying informed, having discernment and recognizing truth over lies. Even in my personal life, the battle of truth over lies was very much a challenge. Cameron, looking at you.

I flicked on the lights in my Pinterest inspired 'self care oasis' and the entire space illuminated into a soft golden glow. Every time I walked into my spa room, actually any room in my house, I admit I was still a little bit in awe. I'd done pretty well for myself despite everything else. I was happy to indulge my inner artist, with all of the latest trends in home goods and furniture. This was a passion that I had held since childhood, and it felt so good, deep in my soul, to go a little crazy and over budget to create my dream home. Finally.

I click on Spotify and hit my morning praise song and rejoice, "Won't He do it?" I have so much to be grateful for, even if everything isn't exactly going my way at the moment, I am grateful.

I turned on the faucet and grabbed my toothbrush to start my morning ritual, and I stuck my head out to watch what was happening in the world today. I finished my morning Mary Kay routine, the anti-aging line, because my God-sister stands by this brand, and she is always glowing. Next I add a light glaze of La Mer to my arms and legs. J-LO swears by it and she is fab at fifty. I'm ready to rock.

"You're going to find love, Ava," I told myself as I read the affirmations I posted in yellow sticky notes alongside the left side of my mirror. "And it's going to be everything you dreamed of, and more!"

I smiled at my reflection. *Above and beyond. All that you can ask or think. This will be an amazing year.* Just think of how far you've come girl, so don't lose faith now.

To be three weeks from forty, I did a fairly decent job of taking care of myself. I didn't look a day over thirty, and that was saying something since I rarely made significant time to enjoy the self care I deserved over the years due to working so much. Sitting in my sauna or hot tub after a long day of work was pleasant, but what I really needed was more spa days and pampering in my future. More vacations, more wellness retreats, more me-time. To just be. Just be Ava.

"This year will be different," I whispered, reassuring myself.

I heard my phone ring as I rotated to turn the shower on. I didn't have to guess who it could be, seeing as though the only person crazy enough to call me this early was Vera Richards. I grabbed my phone to see the selfie I'd taken of us last Easter on the screen. From the outside looking in, we appeared to be the perfect mother-daughter duo. And on most days, we absolutely were. I knew my mom loved me, adored me and protected me with a fierceness that could only be described as a tiger mom. No matter what happened, she was thinking of what's best for Ava, and instinctively she put my well-being above her own needs, which often made me feel guilty, but oh-so-thankful to have an amazing mother. Not everyone is so fortunate, and I have always known what a rare treasure it is to have a parent that loves unconditionally. However, there were those days when we still would butt heads, like any mother and daughter. I was stubborn and didn't listen, and she was opinionated and always right. Cameron, of course, just had to prove that part to be true. Can't say I wasn't heavily warned that I was wasting my precious time.

I pressed the answer button. "Good morning, Mother," I said, trying to sound cheery. But first, coffee!

"Ava!" she shouted. Loud. Like all the Richards.

I bent my head away from the phone, to get some relief for my ear. My mother was the only person I knew who was this lively at five o'clock in the morning. "Mom, why are you shouting my name this early in the morning?"

"Because I just came up with an absolutely amazing and perfect idea for your fortieth. Darling, you are going to love this! We are going to celebrate! Ha!"

Dear God, what is it now? I pulled the phone away from my ears, and took a deep breath. Chances were I was going to regret my next question.

"What is it? I'm listening," I informed her while walking towards my kitchen. I was sure a super-sized coffee was needed for this conversation.

"Do you remember Evelyn?"

"Who?" I asked.

"Evelyn Downing, she goes to my church," she insisted.

I leaned onto my island. I felt I knew where this was heading and

8

quickly realized I was right to regret asking. I rubbed my fingers against my temple. It was too late to back out now.

"No, Mom, I don't remember her. Why?"

"Well, she has a son who just retired from the Air Force. We were talking after service last week, and she was telling me about how he just retired and landed this job at Harrington Technology. Now, I know that you haven't been on a date since Cameron, so I told her about you."

I rolled my eyes.

As if my love life wasn't pathetic enough, my mother thought meddling and hooking me up with a random stranger was a good idea. A random stranger that was old enough to be retired, at that. What did I do to deserve this?

"I'll pass," I replied sharply.

"What do you mean you'll pass? Ava, for heaven's sake, you're almost forty and never been married. If you don't start entertaining prospects now, you're going to be an old maid. And no one wants to marry an old maid."

I swallowed my discontent with her observation and slight insult. It's too early for my mother to be doing her psychobabble marriage PR on me. Not to mention, this would only lead to me saying something that pisses her off for a few days. One would think being a therapist, and someone who constantly shoved relationships down my throat, she'd understand that now is just not the time. Obviously.

"Mom," I sighed. "Is this really what you called me this early in the morning to talk about? A blind date with a stranger? What about 'stranger danger' or is that not a thing anymore? Because when I told you I met an interesting man online, you hit the roof."

"He's a really nice guy, Ava. He is *very* accomplished, he is kind, and he wants to get married. I repeat, and listen carefully dear, he *wants* to get married. This is not Cameron, okay love. This is a grown man that wants a wife. He will appreciate you for the beautiful woman you are, and he will match you in every way. Evelyn and I have already discussed, so don't give me no problem today! " she protested.

"No. Nope. Not today. Mom, I'm sorry but I am not desperate enough to date someone my mother is trying to hook me up with, just because I'm turning forty. Let alone someone I've never seen before, a total stranger, what is the point? Are you trying to embarrass me?"

"Oh, sweetie, you passed up desperation five years ago." Did she really just say that? Ouch. My eyes widened in sync with my jaw dropping at her bluntness. "At this point, you need to grab hold of the best candidate you can snag and settle down."

My mother's tough talk had no bounds. I was gutted by the words but I also had to question, do mothers know best? What if I don't play the game, start dating again on all the apps, get myself "out there," then what? Ava, perpetually alone, is not at all what I envisioned for my forties and forever after.

I slammed the coffee creamer down on the counter. My mother could get under my skin and push my buttons like no one else. Who was the famous person who said, "of course your mother can push all of your buttons, she installed them!?" Brilliant.

She spent so much time trying to marry me off and I never understood why she couldn't trust that love would eventually find me. Sure, she had a great career, degrees, husband and kids, and she was generally fulfilled. Her timetable was different from mine, but she had managed to have it all. Why she couldn't see that of course I wanted the same was irritating, but I wasn't interested in being set up. I wanted more than a quickly arranged wedding, more than just to have a husband-on-paper and a ring to show off at Sunday service, I wanted real and lasting love.

"If you're suggesting *once again* that I settle down, you can stop now because that isn't going to happen. When the right man comes along, I'll know. Until then, I will continue to enjoy my freedom."

She huffed. "Freedom is overrated. The same goes for being an independent woman. We need men like they need us. I curse the day the feminist movement made headway."

Wow.

I shook my head. My mother was a walking contradiction at times. Turning her nose up at the very movement that opened doors for her to obtain her education and the illustrious career she's had. She was always at the forefront of anything to do with civil rights in our city.

KCAL5 had her on the second Sunday of every month to give "local opinion" and provide commentary on issues related to the unhoused and marginalized citizens. Everyone knew Vera could be counted on to show up and support any fundraiser in town, with my Dad's checkbook wide open, unless the event unfortunately happened to be scheduled on a tournament day. Please don't ever attempt to get between Vera and her tee-time.

The scent of the hazelnut beans was comforting. I slowly inhaled the aromatic notes of the caffeinated drink I desperately needed this morning and glanced at the clock on my microwave.

"Really? Isn't the feminist movement the very reason behind you being so successful? Mom, you had a career *and* a family. Why are you always so insistent about me getting married?"

"Because, Ava, we weren't created to be alone. Check your Bible." Basically, checkmate. How do you argue against that?

"Have you ever considered maybe I don't want to get married?" I asked in a serious tone. "I'm just saying, perhaps marriage isn't something I aspire to do." Not at all true, but buying time. And if it happens to be slightly annoying to my mother, well maybe that's bonus points. Hey, I liked to tease her right back and ruffle her feathers too. We had a little gag that we did.

"Poppycock, Ava! Every woman wants a husband," she chastised me. "We all want security and to come home to something other than an empty house."

But it's my house. I paid for it. "I wish you would celebrate my accomplishments as much as you did Amber's."

"You should be more like your sister. She went to college, found her husband, and settled down. At the rate you're going, her kids are going to be my only grand kids. I want more grand kids Ava! You alone can make that happen."

I rolled my eyes to the ceiling. No pressure, then? This time was harsher than the last time. Grateful that she didn't Face Time me. She would've seen, plain as day, how I *really* felt about Amber's life choices. Amber was my younger sister, the second oldest, and my mother's golden child. If Suzy homemaker was a millennial, she'd be Amber. As long as I can remember, Amber wanted the husband, the kids, and the white picket fence, which made my mother's eyes glow with joy and pride. I, on the other hand, chose to be established financially before I made demands from another person.

I also didn't see any point in Amber spending a whole five, not four, years at a university to get a degree so she could sit at home all day. Amber seemed to love her stay-at-home mom life, but I know myself well enough to know that I would go nuts. Just cleaning and checking homework and cooking casseroles? No ma'am. Not for me.

I really wanted to get through to my Mom that I have made the right choices, for me at least, but I am not entirely convinced either, so let's consider my brother: "Well, seeing as though Andrew is about to get married, that should hold you over for a while."

The hissing sound she made in my ear evoked a chuckle. I covered my mouth and laughed silently in my palm.

Andrew's future wife was something else. She checked off all the boxes on my mother's 'no way in hell' list. Andrew was finishing his residency at USC, and she was an aspiring actress and model. Andrew attended church at West Angeles, every communion Sunday, despite his crazy work schedule, but she slept in because of her very late nights as a bartender at Cruzan. Literally, the opposite of everything my mother hoped for in a daughter in law, but guess what? I liked her. She was sweet and she absolutely adored my brother, which is all that mattered to me.

"You can be sassy all you want, but that won't get you a husband," she reiterated.

"I'll be fine," I assured her.

There was a brief pause and I hoped it was her getting ready to end this call.

"Have you heard?" she asked out the blue.

Her tone shifted from cynicism to concern. And I heard the endearment as the question left her lips. I squeezed my eyelids shut. While it's too early for her matchmaking attempts, it was certainly too early for this conversation. This was the last thing I cared to discuss with her.

"Heard what?" I asked nonchalantly.

"Ava, I know you know. You spend more time on that social media crap than anyone I know."

Then why ask? I sighed. Admitting to my mother that I had been somewhat keeping tabs on my scandalous ex was not something I'd be confessing this morning. Yes, of course, I knew he'd gotten engaged, but she didn't need to know that.

"Mom, are you going to tell me what you're talking about? If not, I need to start my morning. I have a few meetings today then I'm meeting Jade later."

"Ava, you and Jade spend way too much time together. You're just two people shy of being the Golden Girls."

This conversation was going nowhere. "She's my cousin. Is there someone else you'd prefer I spend my time with?"

"I won't answer that since you get upset when I do. However, I was referring to Cameron."

Duh, I thought. "What about him?"

She groaned loudly. "He's engaged!"

"And I needed to know that, why?"

"You missed your chance. I told you that you should've given him another chance when he begged for your forgiveness."

My entire face contorted.

"That was never happening. I passed up desperation five years ago, remember?"

"Relationships aren't perfect, young lady."

"You'd know all about that wouldn't you?" Sometimes I was still resentful about my dad, and I hated to be disrespectful but once the words slipped out, I could only feel regret. My mom did everything for me, and yet I still felt this bizarre loyalty to defend my dad. It's not fair, but no one promised children of divorce anything anyway.

I clenched my fists as soon as the statement left my lips. I bit down on my knuckle waiting for her to reply. Her deafening silence let me know I struck a nerve. I stopped midway towards my chaise lounge.

"I'm sorry, Mom. I didn't mean any disrespect."

More silence.

"Mom…"

"It's fine, Ava. I only want what's best for you," she confessed, "but I see you can't see that."

We were now entering the guilt trip portion of the conversation. This is usually when my siblings and I made our graceful exits. She called me, started poking at me, then got upset when I threw it back her way. Psychology was unequivocally my mother's calling.

"Listen, I have to get ready for work. Busy day today. How about we pick this up a little later?" I asked, hoping she would oblige.

"Fine, but consider what I said. He's a nice man and I believe you two would hit it off."

"I'll think about it," I lied. "Bye, Mom. I love you."

"Love you more." And she hung up.

I tossed the phone onto the cushion. This was not how I wanted to start my morning, being solicited for a blind date. The sound of the coffee machine brewing brought me back. I inhaled the scent and exhaled my frustration. I dropped my shoulders and moved towards my bedroom. A hot shower and some upbeat music were calling my name.

Chapter Two: Here's to Second Chances

The day was almost over. It'd been full of meetings and launch prep. Enough to keep my mind occupied, but I was distracted. My mother's comments circulated throughout my mind as I watched my staff move past my door. My company was in the process of purchasing an up-and-coming tech company and we were on the cusp of launching a new app. On days like this, it felt as if someone was pressing their finger on the fast-forward button and the hours were just speeding by. Even with all of that, I couldn't get our conversation out of my head.

Although most of it was completely uncalled for, I couldn't help but come to terms with some of it being true. Forty was by no means *old*, yet let society tell it, I was past my prime and circling the 'middle aged' drain when it came to settling down and having children. Though when I thought about people who did it early or alone, I wondered if the path I took was a better one. My real hang-up was that I didn't want to struggle, or for my child to suffer because of not having two loving and supportive parents.

Then there was the whole jumping the broom factor. In retrospect, I couldn't confidently say I was ready ten or fifteen years ago. I thought I was. Cameron too, but he proved that to be incorrect. Then there was Lauren. She'd gotten married and had kids with someone who was the complete opposite of marriage material. Trent was the prototype for the exact type of man that a woman should *not* marry, and our friendship suffered because of it. Olivia was in the same boat. Now my brother was freshly engaged, and not a single family member had any hope of that union lasting. All of their situations caused me to struggle with if 'happily ever after' was a real possibility, or just a figment of my imagination.

"Boss," my assistant snapped me out of my thoughts.

"Yes, Ella." I looked up. "Everything okay?"

"Oh, of course, everything is fine. Everyone is starting to pack up for the day. We're headed to happy hour and wanted to know if you cared to join us. We're going to *Tom Tom*. Did you want me to save you a seat?"

I mulled over her offer then looked at the time on my computer. It read 4:30 p.m. We had thirty minutes before we closed. I had a strict rule about everyone being out of here by five. Even if I didn't have much of a personal life, other people were entitled to enjoy theirs, and there was more to life than work. Unless it was absolutely necessary, I rarely required that my team work late. I never wanted to be one of those companies that kept people at work all day and night.

Happy hour with the team did sound really fun, but I had other plans, and I needed to clear my head. "Not this time, Ella, but thanks for the invite. If you guys are done with everything, go ahead and call it an early day. See everyone tomorrow."

She smiled graciously. Actresses truly made the best assistants, because no matter how annoying the job, they knew how to beam positivity and keep the morale up in the office. Ella was indispensable to the office, a laidback Gen Z kid with fresh ideas who arranged the wacky social events which kept everyone coming back, day after day, despite the chaos of our perpetual start-up culture. In exchange, we overlooked her extended lunches, constant non-work related texting, and late arrivals on audition days.

"Thanks, boss. I'll let everyone know." I nodded as she left to let everyone know they could head out early.

I wiggled my mouse to wake up my computer and clicked on my Instagram icon. I typed his name in the search bar, hovering my mouse over his name, contemplating if I wanted to indulge in a bit of self-torture. Obliging my nosy side, I clicked it. His profile popped up revealing the crushing post my mother called me about this morning. The same post I saw days ago. After our conversation, I realized during my shower that this was the real reason she called. It was also her motivation behind trying to hook me up with her church friend's son.

I opened the picture he posted with her hand inside of his, showing off the decent sized diamond ring he'd purchased her. I read the caption I'd read multiple times once again.

I didn't know true love until I met you.

I didn't know true love until I met you?

What? The Actual?...

A tinge of raw jealousy crept up and swept over me for a few seconds, my neck flashed red hot and I could feel a tiny trickle of sweat run from the inside of my bra down to my belly button. His heartfelt, if corny, sentence tugged at my heart strings in the worst possible way. I knew he probably didn't mean any harm to me, but it still stung. We'd spent years together—I thought we were each other's true love—he was mine. Yet it seemed now that wasn't the case. How?

Cameron and I had gone through a lot of growing pains. Most people did when they dated in their twenties. He was my first *real* relationship. I'd hoped he would've been my last, but life didn't work out that way.

Neither did his loyalty, I thought.

I scrolled down the hundreds of comments he'd gotten congratulating them. According to my deep dive, they'd been together a year...*one year* and he knew she was 'the one.' Completely discrediting his theory that he needed more than a few years to know if someone was *the one.* I tapped the mouse on the tag icon and selected her name to open up her page. There were tons of pictures of the two of them, including their engagement announcement. I hit the back button to go back to his page.

Damn, he still looked good. I bit my lip, surprised to be feeling a pang of attraction, despite everything.

Almost better than I remembered. The last time I saw him was three years ago when he called and asked to meet. Initially I was apprehensive about meeting him, but I indulged in my curiosity. That and my mother coerced me into hearing him out. As it turns out, he wanted a second go at making us work. For a split second, I considered it. I'd made it to the point in my career where I could step back and do the family thing without my business suffering, but something in me just couldn't do it.

I had forgiven him, but a part of me couldn't forget everything he'd done. It would've been easy to go back to the familiar, real easy; however, I couldn't shake the feeling I would never fully trust him again. Perhaps, he had changed. Maybe he'd gotten all of it out of his system; nevertheless my intuition kept nudging me. The voice in the back of my mind told me to move on.

So I did.

And clearly he did too. Damn his timing, too. Did he *really* time this sudden engagement, just before my fortieth birthday? Does that mean he is sending me a signal of some sort, like a Last Act clearance tag at Macy's, or is this just some cruel parting shot?

I glanced at the clock that now read 5 p.m. Although I didn't mind if the team left early, I almost never did. Ella liked to tease me that I was a robot, so predictable as if I had put Gorilla Glue on my schedule, and

I should learn how to go with the flow sometimes. I thought that way too in my early twenties.

Somewhere out there was a perfect martini and a glorious charcuterie board with my name on it. I picked up my phone to text Jade that I was finally heading out. She texted two hours ago that she was off, so I knew she was probably already two shakes in the wind with drinks.

Ella tapped the glass.

"Later, boss. I'm headed out for real this time," Ella announced, peeking her head inside my office. "You sure you don't want to join us?"

I smiled. "No, but thanks though. I have plans. Tell everyone I said enjoy themselves, use the company card for the tab and make sure that y'all get home safe."

"Will do, thank you!" She nodded eagerly. "See you tomorrow." I knew opening up the company tab would make everyone's night, allow the drinks to flow freely and surely a few would order some extra food for takeout. I remembered my days as an 'Account Manager' when I had to hustle and think on my feet to get the bills paid on time. As long as no one was taking ridiculous advantage, I was pretty lenient as a boss because I remember the leaner times and the grind of entry level jobs.

"See you tomorrow, Ella."

She waved and then disappeared. I took one last look at Cameron's page before closing out of all my tabs and shutting my computer down. He had clearly moved on, and it was time I did as well. I stood up, grabbed my things, and called it a (long) day.

* * *

"Girl, your mom did what?" Jade shouted over the music. "Auntie Vee, stay on one for real." Her infectious laugh incited me to join in before I took a sip of my martini.

"Hmm, tell me about it. And at five in the morning at that. The whole time she was talking, I held the phone up, staring at it like *seriously*?"

Jade shook her head at my mother's classic pushy tactics. I didn't have to do much convincing since she knew her as well as I did. Unlike my mom, Jade's mother stayed out of her personal affairs. Auntie Janet always said about marriage that she could take it or leave it, but in fact she and Jade's dad were celebrating their 40th anniversary soon, so there's that. Auntie Janet was a fan of marriage, but low-key. She always said, if you find the right one, you will know, and nobody can talk you out of it. Auntie also said, if anyone has to talk you into it, he's not the one for you.

And so Jade dated freely and it was as simple as that. No mad dash to get her down the aisle. If only we were all so lucky.

"I think it's the five in the morning that's got me shook," she said, smirking. "Who wakes up with matchmaking and blind dates on their mind? How excited did she presume you were going to be about that?"

I shrugged. "Beats me. It wasn't until I got in the shower and fully awake that it all made sense to me."

"What?" Jade sipped her cosmo. (I once tried to tell her to move on to a cocktail that's more *on trend*, but she isn't one to live for what people think, at all.) Now, I was hesitant to tell her this bombshell news. Mostly because I knew what her reaction was going to be, we were actually best friends, and we didn't keep secrets. She might've been my first cousin, but our relationship went beyond blood, we were more like sisters actually. So alike, in so many ways that we could read each other's minds and finish each other's sentences.

"Her reason for calling me, at the crack of dawn today."

"Which was?"

"Cameron." I reached for my glass, waiting for her reaction. I took a long sip of my drink, while watching her face go from relaxed to annoyed. Jade was in no way a fan of his after he took me through the ringer. "He's getting married apparently."

She arched her eyebrow. "Whaaa?...Apparently?"

"Yeah, he posted it on Instagram. Guess he's capable of real commitment after all." My voice cracked just a little at the end, and I know she caught it.

Her forehead furrowed at my sarcasm. She leaned back and crossed her arms. The remark came off a tad more bitter than I wanted it to. Her facial expression was proof of it.

"And this bothers you?"

"Is that a rhetorical question or an actual question?" I inquired.

"Depends. Does it bother you that he's moved on?"

I pondered over her question. I could lie and say it didn't, but she'd see straight through me, so I opted for the truth instead. "A little...I guess I didn't expect him to *actually* move on."

She leaned forward, and stretched out her hands towards me. "But that's what you wanted right? You told me yourself you didn't think you could ever trust him again. If that's the case, then what's the problem?"

Her line of questioning gave me pause. She probed further than expected. I didn't foresee us getting this deep at happy hour. But she had a point. He did come back, and I told him no.

"No problem, I guess..." I paused. "It's just... I've been questioning a lot of my past decisions, the closer I get to my fortieth birthday."

Jade placed her hand on top of mine.

"Ava, if you don't listen to anything I tell you, listen to this. Life is way too short to live with regrets. What happened with Cameron is over. You had a chance to go back, and you decided to go *forward*. You chose *you*. Don't beat yourself up over that. There's so much more life to live, so live it."

Her words touched me. She was right. Life was too short to live with regrets. I made my choices when it came to love and my career—I couldn't go back. Dwelling on those decisions was pointless, regardless of what my mother said. I looked around the room, then suddenly, I was hit with a fresh idea, and a burst of inspiration and creativity landed.

"You're right, Jade. Speaking of which, you just gave me an idea."

"Do tell," she said.

"I can't rewind time with Cameron. What's done is done, but I don't want to move into this next era of my life with any regrets, so I'm going to change that."

She gave me a perplexed look.

"I mean you have me on the edge of my seat with the suspense here, Ava. You want to speed this revelation up."

We laughed.

"Calm down. So, I've been thinking about my oldest friends these past few weeks, and I was thinking that maybe for my birthday, I'd plan a special trip and invite them to join."

She frowned. "That's not what I was expecting you to say."

"What were you expecting?"

"Not sure, but that wasn't it."

"I miss my friends." I sighed. "Aside from you, I don't have anyone to hang out with. I love everyone I work with, and that's cool, but I can't let loose and hang out with them, obviously."

"Well, make new friends, Ava." Her advice came off snarky even though I know that wasn't her intention. "Besides, we have the only crew we need right here, am I right?" Jade lifted what was left of her cosmo, to cheers with me.

We giggled playfully, because we know the times we had to be each other's only supporter and confidante. The first day at a new school. Summer camp. All of the times that we locked arms and forged ahead, knowing that we had family if nothing else.

"You're everything and more, my dear sis, but seriously...I miss them."

Jade stared at me with that face she always made when she was trying to read my mind. Her expressions softened when she saw my confession was sincere.

"Aw girl. I understand. You all were so close at one time, and the fall out was always weird to me; still, they were your best friends. Therefore, if they're who you want to spend your birthday with, go for it. But please don't expect me to come along and get along, uh uh, nope."

Relief passed over me. I knew that took a lot for her to say. Especially since she was the one who had always been there to help me pick up the broken pieces of my life and failed friendships.

"Thanks, Jade, I know you aren't their biggest fan," I teased.

"Not in the least bit, but you have to do what's best for you. I just hope they don't blow you off."

Me too.

"I'm going to reach out to them when I get home. I'll call Farrah and have her set up everything up! I'll reach out to everyone after I make the travel arrangements."

She held up her hand. "Wait, don't tell me you're sponsoring this little reunion." The scowl on her face would have made a fabulous meme. I keep reminding myself to snap more photos and run a little video from time to time, for the gram.

"Yes, I don't mind, but I'm not going to tell them that out the gate. I'll extend the invite and see where it goes from there."

Jade gave me a *yeah right* look, and I could see she wasn't onboard with my funding idea. "I don't think you should pay for everyone, Ava, but hey, it's your money. I guess you'll know if they really want to make amends if you don't."

I raised my eyebrow.

"What's that supposed to mean?" I questioned.

"It means your so-called friends have made no effort to reach out. How many years has it been? Not to mention, it's no secret that you have beau coup money. You've been covered by the press for awhile now, Ava, I'm sure they've heard, and let's face it, people talk!"

I had to roll my eyes and acknowledge, that was all too true.

"If they say yes before you tell them you're paying, then cool. If not, then you know where they stand and that they are only coming for the free trip." Jade has drawn a line in the sand and we shall see.

Her comment stung. The excitement I had ten minutes ago was fizzling, but I was still optimistic. I had to be. Lauren, Camille, Olivia, and I were friends way before I became wealthy. I had to believe all that history meant something.

"It's going to be great! Like a sleepover at the beach!" I told her, perking up. "We're going to have so much fun and catch up on life, really talk late into the night and get to know each other all over again. All that past stuff is in the past."

She looked at me with the same look of disbelief.

"Mm hmm," she mumbled. "We shall see."

"That we will."

I raised my glass and toasted to her skepticism.

***

Cameron paused mid-shave and stared at his reflection: *Now I have a hard choice to make- reach out to the one that got away, and lose the one I'm with, or let more months go by and pretend that I'm not still in love with Ava Richards. Meanwhile, the pressure from Ana's peeps is building, and I know deep in my heart of hearts that I can't marry this girl. She's got nothing on Ava. Like for real, Ana didn't even question that even her name is just a placeholder for the original. Ava 2.0 deserves the truth. I can't. She*

25

is surely not an upgrade. Damn.

Ana is yet again bugging me to pay her rent, while Ava is a boss and I'm the fool that let her get away. I hate that I listened to my boys hype me up. When Ava even slightly hinted that she wanted to be married, I should have fallen on my knees. Now there is no diamond big enough to catch her eye, to bring her back around, as surely she doesn't need me for anything. Admittedly, I was low key intimidated that she earns so much more, but hell, she earns so much more than like ninety percent of people. Not being in her life isn't going to change that, so I have to hold it together and come up with a plan.

3

Chapter Three: For the Good Times

I sat on my couch and flipped through my photo albums from high school and college. All morning I had been sipping coffee and reminiscing about old times. I didn't have any plans this weekend other than relaxing and tidying up around the house. I traced my finger over the plastic covering then pulled it back. I removed the photo of the four of us in Hawaii. We looked so carefree. Life was good then. We had no worries, nothing stressing us, just four friends, traveling and enjoying life.

It was our last trip before everything went to hell in a hand basket.

I smiled at the innocence our faces held. Youth had a funny way of leading you to believe things would last forever. Never in a million years did I think otherwise. I flipped the picture over. *Summer 2004* was scribbled on the back. Two years later, Lauren would be welcoming her first child and three years after that, her second. Thinking back to those times, I never imagined she'd be the first one to have kids. But Trent had gotten his hooks into her with no intentions of letting her go.

The other pictures reflected the same amount of fun and excitement. It had been our first girls trip ever. We'd decided that we were going

27

to do the opposite of everyone else on spring break- forget about the overcrowded Miami and Ft. Lauderdale beach scene- and so we headed to Hawaii instead. I slid the picture back in its place and continued to flip through the album. I landed on a picture of us on the beach at sunset.

Page-after-page I laughed, smiled, and reminisced over our experiences. It wasn't long before a wave of sadness swept over my walk down memory lane and Jade's skepticism crept up. I knew she was only looking out for me, but maybe she was right. What if they did blow me off? Was I really okay with them *only* coming if I paid for it?

I sat the photo album beside me, slouched down into my soft velvety couch, and laid my head against the back cushions. Doubt settled inside of my thoughts. We hadn't parted on the best of terms. Almost ten years had gone by. No communication. No meetups for lunch or even a coffee. Not even accidentally bumping into each other, at a convention, or in a mall or an airport. Not a single peep. I wasn't even sure where Lauren or Olivia lived these days, were they still on the East coast even?

"No, get it together, Ava," I told myself, sitting up and shaking off the self-sabotage. "Everything is going to work out."

I took a deep breath, releasing the worry that was wallowing, and picked up my laptop. This was my wish. To spend my birthday with my friends. I had to believe they wanted to rekindle our friendship as much as I did.

My first order of business was to find out where they were located. Afterwards, I could make the necessary travel arrangements. I opened my browser. The last I heard, Lauren was a professor. I wasn't sure where, but if I knew Lauren, I was sure she'd received some kind of accolades. I typed Lauren Pruitt in the search bar. Seconds later, countless articles written about Dr. Lauren Pruitt-Halsey came up.

I had briefly forgotten to search for her by Halsey, her married name, because of course she married Trent. Actually, that was a lie. I didn't forget, I wanted to though. I clicked on the most recent article to see she was a tenured professor at Columbia.

She stayed on the east coast, New York City, not entirely surprised there.

I copied her name, opened another tab, clicked the Instagram icon, and pasted it in the search bar. Unlike most names, hers was unique enough there weren't a ton of other options. Scrolling through her page, she had tons of pictures of herself, Trent, and the kids. I rolled my eyes at the pictures of Trent. Although I had to admit it, he and Lauren appeared to be pretty happy. I saw she added two more kids to the bunch, and I wondered if Trent had done something with his life or if he was still riding her coattails.

He never deserved her. Was I more irritated that he had never come to this realization, or that she didn't?

I moved the page down to confirm she did in fact reside in New York. Once an east coast girl, always an east coast girl. At least in her case. I hopped back over to do the same for Camille. Turns out, she was also living in New York, but had opened an LA office as well. *And she didn't even think to call me. Oh well.*

I searched for her on Instagram too and saw she had started *L'Eventopia,* an event planning business that seemed to be doing quite well. She also had a large following. I clicked her business page. The photos of events she had coordinated were actually quite amazing. Incredible floral designs, over the top walls of roses and canopies of balloons were the hallmark of these gorgeous events, which seemed to be taking over Hollywood. I even saw a few celebrities intermingled among the among pics and I could tell immediately that Camille was now a rising star. Good for her. I felt proud of her success, and happy that things had worked out well for her, finally.

Thankfully all of them had contact information listed on their pages. Now that I had the information I needed, I could plan accordingly.

"Now, where to go, Ava?" I said aloud.

I was torn between Cabo or Turks and Caicos. I'd been to Cabo a few times, and loved it. I hadn't been to Turks and Caicos yet. If I asked Jade, I was sure she'd say Cabo since it'd be the cheaper option. I laughed at the mere thought of her saying, *"Oh hell no, you ain't taking them to no damn Turks and Caicos."*

I picked up my phone and called her anyway. I needed a laugh and some direction.

"Hello," she answered.

"Jade, I need your help."

"Girl, what do you want? You're interrupting my *'me'* time."

I laughed. "I need your advice on something."

"What? Have you already nixed the idea of your reunion tour?"

"You know what..." I laughed at her shadiness. "I can't decide whether I want to go to Cabo, or Turks and Caicos."

She burst out laughing.

"I know you're lying!" she yelled.

I buckled over laughing as she went off in my ear. Jade always made me laugh with her craziness. "I knew you were going to say something crazy."

"Then why did you call me? Girl, bye, I'm not doing this with you today. Goodbye, Ava Richards!"

She hung up and I continued laughing. I scrolled my contact list for my travel agent's name. Once I located it, I tapped her name and hit the speakerphone button. Farrah had been my travel agent for years and I knew she'd point me in the right direction.

"Ava! My dear! Long time no hear. What can I do for you, darling? Have missed our chats."

I loved her accent. Farrah was Nigerian and Italian, so the mixture of her heritage made the way she spoke so dramatic. Most of the words were elongated and she stretched her syllables. Until she got impatient with too many questions from a client, and then she flipped into a native New Yorker.

"Farrah, I'm well. How've you been?"

"Well, darling, well," she said gleefully.

"I need to plan a trip. Actually, I need you, the expert, to plan it for me, and a small group of my girls from my college days. A reunion of sorts."

"Of course, where, on this Ah-mazing planet do you wish to go? And when do you want to depart?"

"That's the thing I need your help with. I can't decide if I want to go to Cabo or to the Caribbean for my birthday."

"Your birthday!" she shouted. "When is your birthday?"

I smiled at her excitement. Farrah carried joy in her voice whenever I talked to her. She almost always sounded genuinely happy. That's where I wanted to be in life.

"It's in two weeks and it's my fortieth," I told her proudly.

"Oh my goodness! We must do something special. So, I'll say this, travel to Turks and Caicos is typically better during February to April. You can still go, but considering just weather and such, for now, for you Cabo is much better—I would recommend Cabo. Besides, I have a hookup to an Ah-mazing villa that you will absolutely adore, my dear! One of my *other* favorite clients has to be abroad in Europe all month, and has made his unit exclusively available to me. Ava, it has the works, I promise you. I think you will love it!"

"Well, Cabo it is then," I agreed, as Farrah has never disappointed yet.

"Excellent! Send me all the deets; who's going and the dates you want to be there, and I'll handle the rest."

"You're the best, Farrah. I'll send everything over this evening."

"Do I need to create separate payment links or one?"

"One is fine. Once you have everything planned, you can charge my card you have on file."

"Perfect! You know Ava, you're such a sweetheart, I hope they appreciate you, my dear. You're one of a kind. Okay, honey. Talk to you soon."

We ended our call and I opened my email to send her the info, along with my requests for this prime private villa on the beach. I only needed to create a menu, and give some directions to the house manager, and everything would be set. Now the only thing left to do was convince my old friends to join me. *Old meaning, from the past, not old as in 'forties.' Aging is and will always be a privilege.*

4

Chapter Four: When All Else Fails

I stared at my nearly empty email inbox. Ella was great about sorting and handling anything urgent, so truth be told, I had very little email to review personally. By the time my coffee cup landed on my office desk, the main agenda items were input to my calendar, my meetings were arranged, and I merely had to review the ad campaigns. The dreaded ad campaign numbers were the most annoying part of managing the media business, but the revenue made it worthwhile.

Three days had gone by since I reached out to my friends with an invitation to join me in Cabo in a week and a half. Farrah had made all the arrangements, there was nothing left to do, all I needed was for them to agree to it. I was trying to remain hopeful but the fact that I had yet to receive a read receipt for any of the emails being opened was disheartening. Best case scenario, it was just a simple oversight, the email went to spam, and they hadn't received it. Worst case scenario, they did receive it and had sent it to the trash. Not bothering to open it at all.

Thoughts of embarrassment ran rampant across my mind. Doubt crept up to the surface. My feelings were all over the place. So many questions and so many regrets were bouncing around in my head that I was developing a mild headache.

Ten years was a lot of time to go by without speaking to someone. Then to receive an invitation to leave the country out of the blue seemed random. I wasn't even sure if any of them had even kept in touch with each other. Were they talking about me? Deciding as a group?

After my conversation with Jade, I decided to leave a little room for disappointment, but I never planned for them to not respond. At all. Ever? Fingers crossed I was at least hoping to get an *I'll think about it,* or a *wow, it's been a minute,* or just a *thanks girl, but I can't make it.*

But nothing...I wasn't expecting that.

I clicked on the sent tab and opened the email I sent to Lauren. Then read it again to make sure it didn't read wrong.

Hey Lauren,

I hope you're doing well. It's been a long time since we've spoken, and I would love to see you again. My birthday is around the corner, and I want to enter into this next era with you! So let's catch up! Our friendship means a lot to me, and I don't want to spend another day without my besties in my life. Let's gather on the beach in Cabo for a week to reconnect and celebrate this next milestone in my life. Let's have a fabulous-at-forty girls trip!

Ava

It didn't really read wrong, I thought. But maybe it didn't read right? I had no idea how to bridge this huge gap in time, but I wanted to reach out and rekindle the friendship, get the band back together. Yes, it felt corny, but I had to try.

I did the same for Olivia. I thought the emails came off as endearing and friendly. At least Ella said so. Initially, I seriously considered that

I should reach out to Camille last, if and when I heard back from the others. It would just be easier that way. Goodness knows I couldn't imagine spending my vacay alone with crazy Camille, but I did sincerely want her there, with the other girls. I looked out into my backyard as I got up to walk towards my hammock. Today was a typical spring day in LA. The sun had started to set which made it cool enough to sit outside, take in the view, and relax.

I nibbled on my bottom lip, contemplating whether or not I should send another email, including the information Jade had advised me not to offer. If I were being real with myself, I was nervous about what would happen if I didn't tell them the trip was paid in full. At the same time, I was worried about the outcome if I did. Ever since Jade said what she said, I'd been apprehensive. Our friendship, strained or not, extended far beyond what we could do for each other. *Hopefully.*

A gust of warm wind blew past me then through the large banana plant leaves and elephant ears that surrounded my patio. The tropical plant varieties the landscapers had planted made me feel like I was in the middle of a rain forest oasis. I sat my laptop on the bench next to my hammock to unhook it and open it up. I glanced around the garden and took in the view of the infinity pool, feeling so grateful for having some private space in this bustling city. This sunset view over the city was magnificent, on a warm night like this one with cotton candy skies. I was always amazed at how serene being out here felt, even in a city of millions.

I rested my head against the built-in pillow and peered up at the sky. The predicament I was in was quite perplexing. I could wait a few more days to see if they responded, but that would only shorten the amount of time they had to get prepared, or I could send another email informing them that all the travel arrangements had been made; they just need to show up.

What to do, Ava?

I squeezed my eyes together with my fingers. I was determined to fix my friendships. Without hesitation, I picked up my laptop again to send another email. This time, letting them know the costs were covered. I toggled between sending a group email, but quickly decided against that. Unaware of their individual relationships, I went with my first option of sending separate emails.

I clicked the compose option and started typing, this time adding the *all-expense paid* information and links to the resort website, to entice them to respond. I proofread the emails and made sure it read how I wanted it to, but didn't sound too desperate, and then I hit send. The pop ups notified me they'd been sent off. I closed my computer and pushed it to the side.

This was it.

If they didn't respond after this email, I would call Farrah and tell her to cancel two of the tickets, switch the other to Jade's name, and the two of us would go. I was all for rekindling past relationships, but what I wasn't going to do was beg anyone for their time or attention. That's where I drew the line. I had feelings too. I knew there were some things from the past I had to make up for, things I could have done or even said differently, but I wasn't completely wrong in what I said, nor would I carry that burden alone. We all said some things that might've been cruel. Same went for our behavior.

That's in the past, Ava.

***

Lauren sat by the window watching the late spring snow fall and questioned the pros and the cons of this unexpected invite. *Hard to believe that I would jeopardize my professorship to take off during exam week for a party, but sometimes you just have to lean hard into self-care right? Vacay by the ocean, with my oldest and best girlfriends, in perfect 85 degree tropical weather, surely beats out the daily grind here, trudging through snow in my Uggs.*

I hate that we have lost touch, that we had some falling out moments, but if that could all be repaired, it would be so amazing to have my girls back in my life. I've missed Olivia and hopefully Camille has matured, and we can get back to the good old days when we were the life of every party. If it means putting up with Ava for a few days, it might be worth it to get to some sun and sand right now. Hard to believe that she is sponsoring this little getaway, but its even harder to believe that so many years have gone by. Wow. We are forty?!

***

I pushed the indifferent thoughts to the back of my mind when I heard a ding. My arm reached for my computer to see what the alert pertained to. Opening it, I saw I had received an email. I checked my inbox to see it was from Lauren.

I exhaled, freeing an anxious breath from my lungs. My finger slid across the keyboard, softly tapping a key to open the email. And there it was in black and white. Her response. Four simple words that stung a lot more than I anticipated.

'Sorry, I'm not interested.'

There was no explanation, no rhyme or reason, just a simple rejection. I wasn't entirely surprised. Lauren and I hadn't necessarily parted on the best of terms. I failed to show up for her during what was a huge moment in her life—and she was still pissed. *Obviously.* My first instinct was to send an equally petty response, but I paused. My fingernails tapped the keys as I thought of something to say. While it would be easy for me to blow her off like she did me; I didn't want to take that route.

My fingers hovered over the compose button. I debated what I would say to her when another email came through.

Camille.

I opened hers to read a similar response, but not an outright no. I read her reply: *I don't know, I'll see, give me a few days.* I immediately turned my nose up. Well, there had always been a little competition between us.

"Whatever," I mumbled, closing my computer. "If they don't want to come, so be it. I'll just celebrate this birthday like I've done all the others—without them."

I rocked myself back-and-forth inside the hammock when my computer alerts rang out again. The rocking ceased as I sat back up to see what it was. Olivia had yet to respond, so it was probably her. And it was. I clicked open her email and forced a smile.

Yes! I'll be there! Can't wait to see you, she wrote.

Guess there was a silver lining after all.

5

Chapter Five: Bon Voyage

Time had flown by quicker than I had expected, but with the business merger being on the cusp of completion, the app launching in another two weeks, and preparing outfits for my trip, I looked up and it was time to go. With everything going on, I wondered if this was a good time to take a vacation. Half of my so-called friend group had declined, so I'd been second guessing it ever since then. And if it weren't for Jade, I would've actually canceled and spent *this* birthday like I had all the others since the split with Cameron—dinner with my bestie, a couple of drinks afterwards, then home to cuddle up with a blanket and Netflix.

But Jade wasn't having it this year. After she let me have my 'woe is me' moment, she tore into me with, *"Ava, get it together! You wanted this so put those big girl panties on and do what you need to do!"* Then she reminded me that it was my fortieth and spending it like the others was out of the question.

A smile formed as her voice echoed in my ear. I stared at my MacBook, trying to finish the last of my work for the day when I caught a silhouette out of the corner of my eye.

"Hey, boss," Ella tapped on my door frame, interrupting my thoughts. "Do you have a minute?"

"Everything OK?" I asked.

"Um yeah, just that I need you to come look at something in the conference room."

I eyed her suspiciously. The mischievous smile and her tone that she tried to disguise seemed questionable.

"You sure?"

"Yeah." She nodded. "Gayle and I set up the campaign for the next project and wanted you to give it a once over before you left so we can finalize it while you're gone."

"Alright, give me a minute and I'll be right there."

Ella raised her arm to glance at her watch.

"Sure thing. And what time are you getting out of here by the way?"

I laughed.

This was her second time hinting around to me about not working the whole day. She was surprised when she saw me darken her office door this morning. Ella was an awesome assistant, and though I had almost fifteen years on her, she often shifted into boss mode when she noticed I was in my workaholic mode. Even though I encouraged a healthy work-life balance with my employees, most times I forgot to apply it to myself.

Guess that's what happens when you don't have a personal life, I thought.

"I won't be here long," I assured her. "Finishing up my last task for the day."

She smiled and nodded. "Good, because you deserve a vacation as much as the rest of us. I promise I'll hold it down while you're gone."

"Glad to hear it. Give me ten minutes and I'll be in there."

"All good," she said, turning to return to the conference room.

I returned to the task I was working on before Ella snapped me out of my daydream. The last thing I wanted was for anybody to call me while I was off. I knew Ella would only reach out if it was an emergency, the same went for the rest of my team. Everyone here was more than capable of working without me being present. My intuition may have failed me in my previous relationship, but I had to pat myself on the back for being a great judge of character when it came to hiring and selecting the best staff. No way we could have grown so fast without great people who were dedicated.

When I got up this morning, I was only planning to work a half day, but as it crept closer to two, that didn't seem likely. Thankfully, my bags were in the car, so I didn't have to go back home. There's no way I would've made it home to grab my bags, avoid traffic, and get to the Santa Monica hangar in time without breaking a million laws in between.

My office phone buzzed. I pressed the button to answer.

"Yes," I said.

"Hey, boss," Ella replied, "You have a call on line one."

"Okay." I hung up and hit the button to answer the call. "This is Ava Richards."

"Ava!" she shouted in my ear. I froze, inhaling deeply, because I immediately knew who it was.

"Hello, Mother."

"Ava, why didn't you tell me you were leaving the country for your birthday?" she asked. Her tone possessed a bit of annoyance mixed with curiosity. "I was planning something for you."

I started to ask her who told her, but I didn't need to. My family was a real-life party line. If I had to guess, Jade slipped up and told her mother and her mother told mine. Next to my mother, Jade's mother was the queen of spilling the tea. Which is why if there was something we didn't want them to know, we swore one another to secrecy.

"I didn't know I had to send out a memorandum when I wanted to take a trip."

She sighed. "You don't, but as your mother, I would like to know where you are. For safety reasons, you know?"

"You're right, Mom. I apologize. My decision was sudden and well...I forgot." I really hadn't, but she didn't need to know that. The truth was I was trying to avoid the speech I knew she'd give me if I told her *who* I was going with.

"Well, I guess I'll postpone my plans until you return."

Something told me to ask what her plans were, but I was hesitant. I couldn't decide whether or not knowing was better than not knowing. "Mom, what are you up to?"

"Whatever do you mean?" she asked. Her reluctance to answer and her tone told me everything I needed to know. "It's your fortieth for heaven's sake. I wanted to do something memorable for you."

I rested my forehead against my palm.

"Okay, Mom, but whatever you're doing, it better not involve setting me up with a man," I reiterated.

The phone got silent for a few moments. *Bingo.* I knew that's what she was up to. I smirked then shook my head. My mother was so predictable.

"Oh, Ava."

"Mm hmm...that's what I thought. Mom, I have my love life under control. I don't need any interference in it."

She snickered. "If by *under control*, you mean non-existent then I guess."

I rolled my eyes.

I completed the last item on my to-do list, clicked out of the plethora of tabs I had open, but not before checking my email one last time. My inbox opened revealing Lauren and Camille still hadn't responded. I had hoped they would change their mind and decide to come. My heart dropped a little. I was looking forward to reconciling any differences we had, making amends and starting fresh. Life was too short to hold grudges. At one point we were thick as thieves. When you saw one, you saw the other three, and now it was like we hadn't spent our entire college years and grown into adulthood together, which made me sad. I really didn't want a sad fortieth birthday.

"Ava, are you listening to me?"

"Yeah, Mom, I heard you—loud and clear."

"What if we all went out together?"

My brow furrowed. I knew she couldn't possibly be suggesting what I thought she was. But knowing the Richards way- to persist until we got we wanted- she was indeed still clinging to the possibility of the blind date. *Ugh!*

"If you're suggesting I go on a date with him while my mother and his mother accompanies us, you must be losing your mind."

"Not a date, dinner. There's a difference," she insisted.

"It's not and no," I responded firmly. "Mom, I have to go. I'll call you when I get back and the two of *us, me and you*" I emphasized, "can go to dinner."

"Fine. Enjoy your trip, dear. I'll call you on your birthday."'

"Thanks, talk to you later, I love you," I said.

"And I love you more," she said sweetly, then hung up.

I leaned back in my chair. In less than four hours, I would be away from all of the pressure of my company, from the expectations of family, and just relaxing on a sandy beach in Mexico with a refreshing margarita or mezcal cocktail in my hand. Two days from now, I'd be crossing over into a new decade. There were so many things I wanted to accomplish in this next era of my life. Creating my own destiny was one of those things. I wiggled the mouse to wake my computer up, selected the compose option twice and typed Lauren and Camille another email—this time I attached the travel information to it and closed it out. Perhaps they'd have a change of heart.

Wishful thinking, I thought, exiting the browser.

My desk phone buzzed again.

"Yes," I answered.

"Hey, boss, did you forget about me?" Ella inquired.

"Nope, on my way now," I told her, shutting down my computer.

"Okay." She hung up and I stood to grab my things. Once I approved the files that needed my signature, I was headed to the elevator.

The moment I stepped into the main space, I noticed it was fairly empty, concluding most of the team was still at lunch, or gone for the day. We didn't have set schedules, so people typically scattered about during the day. I also allowed everyone to work one half-day out of the week. My office's set-up was a large open California coastal decor space, with glass walls that divided up the cubes to give it some structure, flow, and lots of natural light. There were large balconies open to all for communal working with an ocean view. Generally, everyone enjoyed coming into the office because it was beautiful, very spacious, and far from a torture chamber. All of my staff enjoyed free gourmet snacks, yoga classes, a nap room, and a mental health consultant on site. I set it up so that our workplace was almost a retreat.

Art and self-motivational quotes were hung throughout the space, accompanied by a few people's personal plants and desk decor. Creativity required a space with light and ease. At least for me it did. Working in a stuffy and boring white-walled box just didn't inspire me.

I rounded the corner to the conference room and the instant they saw me, everyone screamed, "Surprise!"

My jaw dropped as my eyes widened. Here I was thinking most of them were gone and they were waiting to celebrate with me. My cheeks were stuck in place as my smile stretched across my face. Metallic balloons were scattered around the room, people blew through confetti whistlers, others waved handmade, cute birthday signs around. Marcus, the office manager, popped a bottle of Veuve, and everyone cheered.

I walked further into the room, hands covering my mouth, my face registering shock and amusement. "Oh my goodness, I can't believe you all did this for me!"

"Well, Ava," Ella began, "We couldn't let you leave for Mexico without celebrating your birthday. I won't spill the beans on your age," she laughed. "Buuutttt, this next milestone is a big one, so...all of this is for you. We love you, girl!"

Tears welled up in my eyes. The sheer fact they'd done this for me, brightened my day, and lifted my mood. My excitement regarding my birthday had been up and down, not really knowing what I wanted to do, however this made up for it. I sat my purse down in one of the chairs.

"I can't believe you all did all of this," I told them, getting choked up. "I don't know what to say."

They all stared at me with smiles as wide as the 405 on their faces. Their eyes beamed with pride. I looked around as I took it all in.

"Thank you," was all I could muster up as I walked around the room to hug everyone. With each hug, they wished me happy birthday and handed me birthday cards. The appreciation was overwhelming. I finally finished hugging everyone and went to stand next to Ella. "Ella, I can't believe you did all of this."

"*We* did this, and you deserve it, Ava. Several years ago you created this vision and you've taken us all on this amazing journey with you. Some have gone on to be great, while others have stayed here to be great with you. We couldn't not show you how much you mean to us," she said.

"Thank you," I murmured again.

"Anytime. Okay let's cut this cake so you can be on your way. You have to get to the airport," she commanded.

I sat down as Jamison, my lead designer, cut the cake and Ella helped him serve. I opted out of the blowing the candles out portion since we were still just getting past the pandemic. "*No extra germs, please*" was my motto for post-pandemic life and returning to what we hoped would finally be our new normal.

Once everyone had a slice, we laughed and chatted about the clients, and eventually about personal updates and then light office gossip. The tuxedo chocolate cake with mousse and cheesecake frosting was beyond scrumptious. I made a mental note to ask Ella where she got it when I came back, because this would definitely become a thanksgiving staple at the Richards' table.

The way the cake melted like butter on my tongue had me wanting more. Too bad I was headed to the airport; otherwise it'd be packed up and stored in my refrigerator.

Ella grabbed a gift bag and handed it to me.

"Happy birthday! I got this for you, ma'am" Now when Ella calls me ma'am I know she is teasing me. Turning forty doesn't make me *ma'am,* or does it?

I placed the plate on the table. "What's this?"

"It's a little something to help motivate and steer you in this next phase of your life."

I reached into the bag and pulled out a beautiful book with affirmations inscribed on the front. The calligraphy was beautiful along with the graphics. I grinned at how perfectly timed her gift was. It was serious and thoughtful, not a gag gift, but something that she cared about sharing with me. I was touched.

"Wow," I said, turning the pages. "It's beautiful, Ella."

She smiled at my appreciation.

"I'm glad you like it. I'm really big on affirmations and manifesting. These past few years, I've had incredible things happen in my life because of it, and I figured you could use this too. Like I asked for an amazing job, and here I am!" She always took an extra thirty seconds to butter me up, and I had to laugh at that- the job security of it all. "How it works is, just write down what you want this next chapter of your life to be—speak it—and watch it come to fruition."

I stood to give her a hug.

"This was right on time," I whispered, hugging her.

And it was. Whether or not anyone showed up, I was going to spend this time by the ocean, communing with the universe, enjoying nature, and getting clear on exactly what, and who, I wanted in this next chapter of my life.

The flight from Santa Monica to Los Cabos was so short that I barely had time to check my email and prepare to unplug for the week. I flipped past the many "Happy Birthday" messages that were generated by customer apps, to see if anything personal had arrived. Sure, its nice when your dentist and your lawyer 'remember' your special day, and who doesn't want a free dessert with your next order from Olive Garden, but really? It would be nice just to get an email not written by a bot, on my birthday weekend.

I scanned through and found an actual reply from Camille, finally!

Subject: Can't Make It – Professional Duty Calls!

Hey Ava,

Guess what? Girl! I am knee-deep in work right now, planning a killer event that's gonna blow minds. So, unfortunately, I'll be MIA for your fab birthday trip. Trust me, it's legit, not just me dodging tequila shots. Why would I do that?! Trust, my client list is exploding, otherwise I would surely drop everything for a spontaneous escape to paradise.

I can't say all, but my latest masterpiece, is in the works. Picture glamour,

WISH YOU HAD TOLD ME

sophistication, and me, in the boss seat. It will be magical, and your invite is in the mail so plan to head east in the next few weeks, darling.

Sorry, dear, but a diva's gotta prioritize her craft. I know you ladies will miss my flair, but hey, show must go on, right?

Enjoy the bash without me, darling! Celebrate the big 4-0! I can imagine it will feel amazing to reach another decade of life! (I'll find out in December) Pour one out for the event planner extraordinaire and just know I'll be on the other coast missing all you girls so much.

In Glitter and Glam,

Camille

With that reply, I'm not so sure that Camille's presence will be missed at all. Off-putting and borderline offensive, yes, but was I surprised by Camille's haughtiness and diva ways? Never. Some things never change, not matter how much time has passed, leopards don't change their spots, right.

6

Chapter Six: Table for One Please

"Hello, I have a reservation for Richards," I told the hostess. I looked around at the beautiful tropical space and exhaled. Upon setting up my travel arrangements, Farrah insisted I eat at The Alexander on the night I arrived.

According to her, and several food blogs, it was voted one of the world's best places to dine when traveling to Mexico, so I made reservations to try it out. Their website stated that it was exclusive, so I jumped on it. I originally reserved a table for four, but when Lauren and Camille backed out, I changed it to two. Turns out that might've been a bit presumptuous of me. I was glad I'd opted to get a villa on the resort instead of the private mansion I wanted at first, that way I had people to socialize with, if in fact it turned out I would be spending my birthday alone.

"Has your entire party arrived yet?" she asked.

I answered, "No, it's just one tonight."

She smiled as she picked up a menu. "Follow me."

I stuffed my disappointment down. Olivia hadn't arrived yet. The original reservation was scheduled for seven, but then I called to push it back an hour in hopes she would've arrived by then. When I reached out to see where she was, she didn't respond. My first response was sadness. I'd arrived at the conclusion she probably thought about it and changed her mind.

I'd almost slipped into full-blown sulking but quickly switched up my outlook.

While on the plane, I took the time to write a few affirmations down. Surprisingly, it was refreshing to see my wishes in black and white. Over the years I'd been so focused on work goals, I never took the time to set any personal ones. Perhaps that was also presumptuous of me. Believing love would somehow find me on its own—buried under mountains of work.

Stop it, Ava.

I exhaled deeply.

I was doing it again. Doubting myself. The complete opposite of what I was supposed to be doing, totally against what I'd written down on the plane, and I didn't want to do that.

"Love will find me," I affirmed. "This trip will be exactly what it's supposed to be."

"Excuse me?" the hostess said, turning around.

I grinned and casually waved her off.

"Nothing." I smiled. "I was just talking to myself."

"Oh, okay." She placed the menu on the table then pulled my chair out. I sat down and scooted it closer to the table. "Your server will be with you shortly," she told me before walking off.

I slid my clutch in the chair next to me. I closed my eyes briefly and took slow, deep breaths to calm my racing thoughts. *Be in the moment, Ava.* After a few more breaths, I opened them again. The view was amazing. The restaurant was completely open, void of any walls; the night air blew off the ocean as the waves hugged the shore. Gentle crashing sounds were a calming soundtrack to the warm breeze that kissed the trees as it grazed across the palm leaves. The dim lighting that hung overhead glowed in unison with the candles on the tables.

The scent of fresh seafood and charbroiled meat wafted to my nose. Soft notes of jazz echoed throughout from the live band. Movement captured my eyes and diverted my attention to the aerial performers who were entangled in white fabric, high up and in the distance. Aerial performers! Wow, they really went all out in Cabo. My eyes and ears were in sensory overload by the soothing, yet stimulating and pleasing ambiance.

I was so caught up in the show, I didn't notice that my server had approached my table.

"Good evening, Señorita. My name is Joaquin, and I'll be your waiter tonight. What can I get you to drink?"

I replied, "Good evening," as I picked up the menu to skim over the drink options. Usually I'd get a margarita, but I wanted something different. I mulled over their choices as I flipped the pages. Nothing jumped out at me, as I was so distracted.

I tapped my finger on the menu. I was trying to think of something I'd had before, but not often, so that it would be special. Then I decided to ask him for recommendations.

"What would you suggest? I'm drawing a blank."

A grin landed on his lips as if he'd been waiting for me to ask that very question. He tucked his pen behind his ear and asked, "Do you typically like light or dark liquor?"

I shrugged. "I'm open, since I'm on vacation."

He bobbed his head at my reply.

"Okay, hmm...are you celebrating something?"

I flashed him a bashful smile. "My birthday is in two days. I'll be forty."

His eyes jolted open at my confession.

"Eres muy sexy, señorita," he said, puckering his lips and waving his hand back-and-forth.

I laughed at how animated he was. My Spanish was good enough that I understood what he said. His facial expressions and compliment were flattering. I felt kind of blah when I first arrived, but he was slowly changing that. I lowered my head to hide the blushing grin I had plastered across my face.

"I have the perfect drink for you then." He seemed confident in his selection. The way his face lit up thinking about it enticed me. I was all in at this point.

I winked at him. "Surprise me then."

Once he hurried off, I went back to perusing the menu. At the bottom of it was Chef Ellington engraved in shiny, beveled print. The name sounded somehow familiar. The menu was extensive, and I was torn between seafood or a steak. The aromas that floated through the restaurant caused my mouth to salivate. I gazed back at the dinner performance. The flexibility of the gymnast left me awestruck. I'd always been fascinated at how gracefully they were able to move their bodies with such ease, while twirling upside down in the air. As my eyes moved across the room, I caught the eye of a gentleman staring at me.

His eyes zeroed in on me while he sipped his drink.

I gave him a partial smile and prayed it didn't prompt him to come speak. Oftentimes the smallest gesture emboldened men. I broke our stare-off to look back down at the menu. My stomach growled, alerting me to put some food into it before I filled up on liquor. The last thing I wanted was to be drunk and alone.

As I decided on what I wanted to eat, my waiter started walking towards me with a goblet filled with a red-orange drink—garnished with a lime and a red chili pepper. I stared in utter fascination at what moved towards me.

He placed the glass down in front of me, smiling like he'd done a great job. I appreciated his enthusiasm. "And what do we have here?" I asked.

"It's called a Vampiro. Our signature cocktail here at The Alexander. I promise it tastes as delectable as it looks."

"I'm intrigued," I replied playfully. He was right, it looked delectable. I wanted to ask him what was in it, but changed my mind. I wanted to experience and sort through the flavors on my own.

"Are you ready to order?"

He pulled his notebook from his apron and removed the pen from behind his ear. I rambled off what I wanted, and he disappeared into the kitchen once again. I lifted the glass to my lips the instant he vanished, moaning internally at the combustion of flavors saturating my tongue. I tasted sweet, spice, a tinge of sour, but definitely alcohol.

I reached for my clutch and took out my phone. I had to snap a picture of this to send to Jade. This might be my new drink for the summer. I snapped the picture then texted it to her. She would be happy to know I arrived safely and was now relaxing. Afterwards I opened my browser to see what all spirits this drink entailed, and while I was reading the ingredients, I noticed the man at the bar get up.

My eyes were glued to my phone as I silently mumbled a prayer that he wasn't headed in my direction. I was all for meeting new people, engaging in riveting conversation—just not tonight. It was my first night and I wanted to take in everything without feeling like I was on the menu.

I sighed the closer he got to me.

"Well hello, beautiful. Are you dining alone this evening?" he inquired.

Slowly, I shifted my attention from my phone to him, and took in the sight of him up close. He wasn't bad looking, but not necessarily my type either. He'd gotten a nice tan on his bronzed skin which meant he'd either been here a few days or he'd been traveling quite a bit. As luck would have it, his tan also revealed the missing wedding ring he'd conveniently removed. I was hesitant to answer since he was a complete stranger. The last thing I wanted was to end up on a missing person's poster or have a friendly vacation stalker following me around for the whole trip.

The world we lived in was not like it used to be. A single lady should be quite cautious. Vacationers, especially women, were prey to the wrong person. I compiled my faux story and said, "Thank you. And just this evening. My friends got in kind of late."

I made sure I used *friends* in plural form so if he was on the prowl—I wasn't an easy target.

"Do you mind if I join you?"

I gritted my teeth. Internally groaning as I chastised myself for holding his attention as long as I had. He'd been sitting at the bar waiting for someone he could approach, and I was the unlucky individual. I shuffled between being friendly and wanting to be left alone. He'd be the only non-service human interaction I had tonight though if I did allow him to sit with me. He stood patiently waiting for my response.

"Will your wife have a problem with that?" I baited him, wanting to see what his reaction would be. And like I suspected, he froze like a deer caught in headlights. "I thought so. It was nice meeting you, but I'd prefer the company of a non-married man. I don't like drama."

He paused, raised his eyebrows in surprise and then nodded at my request and walked off.

I wasn't sure where his wife was, if she was here at all, but I didn't want to find out. I took another long gulp of my drink. With each sip I tasted something different, something wildly better. The savory beverage was becoming a new favorite of mine.

Joaquin reappeared with my dinner. The seared lamb chops appeared to be cooked to perfection. I could smell the fruity scent from the mango salsa that decorated the plate. The bright green asparagus had just the right amount of char, and steam floated off the truffle mashed potatoes as the slice of butter melted down the sides. Everything looked so deliciously mouthwatering.

"Gracias," I said to him.

"De nada. Una mas?" He pointed to my almost empty drink.

Why not, I thought. Might as well celebrate myself. I was on vacation, and I only turned forty once. I lifted the glass to my lips to finish the last few sips and handed it to him.

I nodded. "Si."

7

Chapter Seven: Dawning of a New Day

5:30 a.m.

The room phone rang, shaking me out of my alcohol-induced slumber. I had forgotten I requested a wake-up call before dinner. At the time, getting up to watch the sunrise seemed like a good idea. Not so much right now. I'd downed three Vampiros, two shots of tequila, and a glass of champagne before the night was over. And I was paying for it now. I wasn't in my twenties anymore and my body was reminding me of it. Not to mention I had broken my pledge to myself to stay sober and stay safe. Thank God this resort was high end with security staff everywhere. But still, I had been foolish, on day one.

"Argh," I groaned, rolling over to silence the loud ringing. I tried reaching for the receiver without opening my eyes, but it was no use. My arms weren't long enough and the fact I wasn't in my actual bedroom kept me from knowing where everything was. I finally gave into the noise, cracked my eyes open, and picked up the phone.

"Hello," I answered, with a very creaky and groggy voice. I could not remember the last time I felt this hungover.

"Good morning, this is the wake-up call you requested," the operator said cheerfully.

"Mm hmm," I groaned.

I didn't have nearly as much energy as she had right now. Considering the state I was in, I wholeheartedly understood how people who weren't morning people felt around those who were.

"Have a great day," she said.

"Okay," was all I could manage before placing the phone back on the hook.

I rolled over onto my back. My body felt heavy, my stomach was bubbling, only adding to the throbbing my head was doing. I wanted to get up, I just didn't have the strength. I told myself I had a few more days to catch the sunrise, today didn't have to be the day, but it was my birthday eve and I wanted to set my intentions for this new chapter of my life.

The cool air from the large ceiling fan brushed against my skin. I inhaled several deep breaths before exhaling them. The soft duvet cover contained the perfect amount of weight to keep me cool and comfy without breaking out into a sweat. If nothing else, Mexico held true to its heat reputation. I'd taken the largest room with several large windows upon arrival, considering I was alone and probably would be the entire trip since Olivia never responded.

Up until my third or fourth drink, I was genuinely concerned about her. I didn't know if something had happened to her or not. I started to send her a snappy text but decided not to. People had every right to change their mind. Besides, it was *my* birthday, not theirs.

I rolled over to face the window. The sky was starting to open up and I could see tiny rays of light. I tossed the cover to the side, fully exposing my nakedness to the dark room, before willing myself off the plush mattress. All I needed to do was throw something on, grab my affirmations journal, and drag myself to the patio.

When I first planned to get up so early, I was going to sit on the beach and watch the sun come up. That was pre turn-up. Post turn-up was me stretched out on one of the lounge chairs, snuggled beneath a blanket, writing and observing as God painted the sky with today's colors.

I sighed to release the frustration I felt at not knowing what was happening with everyone else.

This was harder than I expected, I thought.

Once I had my bearings, I grabbed my glasses that I usually only wore at home off of the nightstand. Contacts were out of the question right now. More than likely I'd poke an eyeball trying to put them in. My clothes were already tucked away in the drawers. It was one of those things I automatically did so I wouldn't spend my entire trip bumping my toes against my suitcase. I opened the drawer to find a large t-shirt and some shorts to slip on in case I felt inspired to walk to the beach.

I pushed the closet doors apart to grab my cable-knit sweater I always traveled with, picked my journal off the table, and was outside before sleep drug me back into bed. The moment I walked onto the patio I was greeted with warmth.

Did I really need this sweater? I inhaled the fresh, morning air. The sound of the turquoise water splashing against the shore was relaxing. I leaned onto the back of the chair, contemplating if I was going to sit down, or go with my original idea of sitting on the sand at the beach. It really wasn't that far from my room. A short walk to be exact.

Sunrises and sunsets were two of my favorite things to witness. Watching the sun come up on the beach was a bucket list item of mine, but I never bothered to get up this early on vacation to view one. Being here alone had prompted me to want to do things differently. Take chances. See the beauty around me. Appreciate the simple things life offers.

Beach it is, I thought, stepping off the patio.

Warm sand covered my feet as I buried them in it with each step. The closer I got to the water, the cooler it felt, confirming why I brought my sweater in the first place. The sky was brightening up as I settled into my space.

I dug my toes in the sand, placed my journal next to me, lolled my head back and closed my eyes. The deep breath that escaped my lips was a heavy one, but it felt good. I was just hours away from a new chapter and it felt promising. I had no idea what forty had in store for me, but I was excited to see what it was. I leaned forward and smiled at the scenery in front of me.

The sky behind me was still dark, but in front it was breathtaking mixtures of yellow and orange, which started to stretch across the horizon beneath a dark blue ocean of night that had begun to disappear, moment by moment. Beneath the multi-colored rainbow sky, the cerulean and teal water glowed. Before my eyes, the clouds illuminated with a fabulous warm light as the rising sun announced the coming of a new day.

Dawn continued to emerge. The sunrise had become even more beautiful as the sun peeked over the horizon. The sky had now become a canvas of colors as reds and deep purples, with the light of the sun shining above with a magenta hue, forming a bridge between the orange and blues. As the sun slowly ascended, the various shades of sky fused themselves together, revealing the first rays of the sun grace the earth. Nature was the most brilliant thing to witness.

Pulling my knees to my chest, I wrapped my arms around my legs and marveled at everything in front of me. I smiled at its magnificence. My eyes danced across the miles of colors. I exhaled slowly, and then inhaled the saltiness from the ocean.

This is simply majestic. Look at God!

I picked up my journal and pen and opened it up. It was time for change, time to speak the change I wanted, and to make room for the universe to let it come to pass.

8

Chapter Eight: Sunny Skies and Temporary Highs

I looked around the pool, and dropped my bag with my towel, book, and phone onto an empty lounge chair close to the swim up bar. Most likely I would soon need to indulge in a small 'hair of the dog' cocktail, just to take the edge off this impending hangover. The humidity was turned all the way up and I figured it was the perfect day to lounge around. After watching the sun come up, I went back to sleep for a few hours. The need to sleep off the rest of the liquor I consumed last night was imperative if I was going to enjoy the rest of the day.

When I awakened to total silence, I knew that I was still alone in the villa. Olivia was nowhere in sight and had yet to respond. I hadn't bothered to contact her again and said a prayer that she was okay. I was determined not to let anything or anyone ruin this trip. As much as I hated to do it, I had to relinquish control.

Jade texted me earlier asking how everything was going and I simply told her everything was good. I came close to telling her the unfortunate truth, that no one had bothered to even show up, but I opted out of the pity party instead. She already wasn't a fan of my friends, and telling her that they had indeed left me high and dry would've only added to her dislike of them. Besides, I proclaimed I wanted this trip to be what it was supposed to be. If it was meant to be a solo trip, so be it. I was an experienced business traveler after all, so this wasn't that unusual for me, being alone. Gazing around the pool, I spotted the resort staff setting up what looked to be an activity for the day near the pool bar.

Perfect. I was starving and food was definitely at the top of my list before I even thought about participating in anything or drinking more Vampiros. As I got situated, I felt someone staring at me. He'd been eyeing me since I sat my stuff down, but I hadn't paid him any mind, looking for somewhere to relax.

Until now, I thought.

I pulled my sunglasses down far enough to peek over them. The delicious looking man was a sight for sore eyes indeed. He held a drink in his hand as he leaned against the pole holding up the cabana he and a few others were in. From where he stood, he looked to be somewhere around six feet tall.

My, my, my.

Slowly, I raked my eyes over his hairless chest that led to his uber defined abs. His caramel complexion highlighted the exceptionally toned arms I knew came from countless hours in the gym. He radiated a whole different level of heat, beneath the sun rays. The tropical print trunks he had on were a bold choice, but he wore them well. I nibbled on my lips as I noticed how smooth and shiny his bald head was. *Mmmm,* I thought. He looked too good for words. Too good to be anywhere other than on the cover of somebody's magazine. His eyes made contact with mine then trailed up and down my body.

The neon yellow swimsuit adorning my body left very little to the imagination. The cut-outs accentuated my curves, by design. I'd worked out most of my adult life and it was times like this that I was able to see my hard work and pushing the plate back had truly paid off. When I purchased this swimsuit, I was feeling frisky and somewhat adventurous, though when it came time to pack it for my trip, I almost left it behind. The way he studied me like his favorite subject in school, I was glad I didn't do that. I flashed him a flirtatious grin, then pushed my glasses up and sat down, extending my legs and freshly pedicured toes to the edge of the lounge chair to get comfortable. Fiddling inside of my bag, I found my Air Pods to pull them and my phone out. I scrolled through my Spotify app until I found a playlist suitable enough for a day at the pool: Best of Beyoncé. Perfect vibes. While scrolling, I noticed a waiter walking around taking orders and considered whether I wanted to eat here or at the bar.

The pool Adonis I kept casually staring at behind my shades seemed to be doing the same to me. There was a nice crowd around them that left me wondering who he might be. A local celebrity? From what I could see, his finger was void of a wedding ring, or indication of one— unlike the man yesterday—still, I didn't get my hopes up. I knew how some married men often moved like single men and had a whole wife at home.

Breaking me out of my lustful trance, the waiter eventually made his way around to greet me. He seemed to be the only one moving around which let me know he was about his money. Most people on all inclusive resorts worked for tips, and it was clear he wanted all of them.

"Hola, Señorita, what can I get for you today?" he asked.

"I'll just take water for now." He nodded. "Can you tell me what type of food they have at the restaurant?"

The fluorescent sign read Indigo Grille. I had a general idea what kind of food they served considering it was positioned at the pool, but I wanted to be sure. The meal I ate last night was mouthwatering, but I didn't want anything so decadent right now. Something light, maybe a salad sounded appealing.

"Right now they're serving lunch options, nothing too heavy. Salads, club sandwiches, burgers, and of course tacos—I suggest the baja taco-grilled fresh Mahi , avocado crema and pineapple salsa, it is very good."

"Hmm...all of that sounds great. Let me think about it?"

He nodded his head.

"Sure, just let me know when you're ready, or you can dine at the bar." He pointed. "It's totally up to you."

"I think I'm going to dine at the bar. Thank you though. And the water is good for now."

I needed to hydrate. He scribbled down my drink request and moved to take the next order. I pressed play on my playlist and shifted into relax mode. The pool was pretty crowded, so I would wait until some of the crowd was tired or cleared out. *Naughty Girl* blasted through my ear as I shimmied in my seat. There was just something about a Beyoncé song that made me feel fun, free, and sexy.

This was one of my all time favorites. I loved how she gave women like me permission to feel sexy and in charge of their lives. Working in a male dominated field often forced me to downplay my femininity, just to receive the same amount of respect and recognition they did. Songs like this always made me want to let my hair down.

Fully enveloped in the song, a shadow suddenly was cast in front of me, blocking the sun. Opening my eyes, I lifted my sunglasses to see the handsome specimen I swapped flirty exchanges with earlier standing in front of me. Staring at him from this angle gave me an even better view of just how sexy he was. The ripples in his abdomen resembled those washboards our ancestors used back in the day. I swallowed hard, hoping he didn't notice the increased pace of my breathing.

Removing one of the Air Pods, I did my best to keep my eyes at the appropriate level, making light eye contact with him. Suddenly, I felt flushed—heartbeat pounding against my chest, heat rushing through places I hadn't felt heat in since Cameron. I wanted to fan myself, but that would have been a dead giveaway to the effect he was having on me. His stance was a balance of cocky and confident.

I grinned at him.

"Hello," I said softly. "Can I help you?"

"Depends," he replied.

I asked, "On what?"

He smiled revealing a set of perfect white teeth. I could've sworn I saw a sparkle flash across them. *He has nice teeth,* I thought. That perfectly straight smile was one of my top requirements when it came to physical appearance. How a person's teeth looked always revealed what their grooming habits were. If he doesn't take care of himself, then he certainly won't be taking care of me. But this man right here, well, he along with that gorgeous smile, instantly checked off one of my boxes.

He pointed to the chair next to me.

I nodded, granting him permission to sit down.

"On whether or not you let me buy you a drink" His voice was sexy, deep, hypnotic. "That is if you drink." He glanced at the glass of water sitting on the table beside me.

I giggled.

"Yes, I drink. I'm trying to rehydrate before starting up again. I had a little too much fun last night ."

"I noticed," he responded.

I pushed my glasses to the top of my head. "Excuse me?"

"You were at the Alexander last night, right? I saw you there."

"Are you a stalker?" I asked playfully, but serious at the same time. "Because if you are, let me know now so I can skedaddle. I don't do stalkers." I pulled back in my chair to show that I might be making moves.

He laughed.

"Do I look like I have to stalk a woman?"

I raised an eyebrow at his question. I knew it was more rhetorical than literal. A shameless grin formed on my lips. Normally I'd be turned off by this display of arrogance, but he possessed a certain amount of sexiness I couldn't resist, or deny.

"I didn't know stalkers had a certain kind of look—" I looked him up and down "—though they might look like you."

He snickered, biting down on his lip, causing me to melt a little more in my chair. At this point, I wasn't sure if it was the sun or him that had me overheating.

Jesus be a cool breeze.

I wanted to lift my leg from the chair, but I was terrified it'd make the sound Velcro made when it got separated. Thank God it was hot otherwise my body would've given me away. Picking up the glass of water that was sweating as much as I was beneath this swimsuit, I took several long gulps, hoping it would cool me down, but it didn't. My body was flushed, and it was because of him...whoever he was.

"Tate," he blurted out.

"Excuse me?"

It was like he could read my thoughts or something.

"My name, it's Tate."

I nodded.

He continued, "I figured you want to know so you wouldn't think I was a stalker."

I chuckled.

"I take it that stalkers don't give out their names, huh?"

He rubbed his hand over the dark stubble extending to each side of his face. There was something about a man with a beard that sent chills down my spine, in the best way. I shook my head slightly to dismiss the naughty images racing across my mind. Hmm, the things I could do with a man like this. I couldn't wait to tell Jade all about this later.

He winked at me. "A woman with a sense of humor. I like that."

"Good to know. My name is Ava, by the way."

He poked his lips out as if he were impressed.

"So, Ava, would you like that drink?"

I considered his offer. I really needed to eat first.

"I'd love one, but I need to eat first. I have a general rule not to drink on an empty stomach."

He glanced down at my flat stomach.

"Yeah, we wouldn't want you to do that. I can have the waiter come take your order if you know what you want," he offered. "They have some pretty good food over there."

"I was actually thinking about eating at the bar."

"That works too. I could join you if you don't mind," he implied, waiting for me to extend him another invitation.

"You're quite forward, Tate."

"Only when I see something I want."

Damn. Yeah that did it.

I took another sip of my water. If he kept this up I was going to hyperventilate. Placing the glass down, I returned my attention to him. "And what is it that you want?"

"To share a meal and a drink with an incredibly sexy woman." His response was bold and direct. "That is if she'll have me."

"How do you know I'm not here with someone?" I inquired.

He leaned against the back of the chair.

"Because...this is the second time I've seen you and you aren't with anyone. If you were here with someone—man or woman—especially a man, they'd be here with you. But they're not, which means you're on a solo trip."

Second time? I gave him a partial smile. His assessment was spot on, making me a tad bit sad, also reminding me that my friends weren't here to celebrate my milestone birthday with me.

"Especially a man?"

He sipped his drink and nodded. "Especially a man. Ain't no way in hell you'd be here with me, walking around like this—" his hand glided a few safe inches away and over my silhouette "—and I'm not on your heels. No way, Jose."

I laughed at him.

"Sounds a bit possessive, Tate. Am I hearing stalking tendences?" I teased.

He shrugged. "Call it what you want, but I'd want the world to know who my woman is. That way no one will get any bright ideas and I have to step outside of myself."

Goosebumps crawled up my arms.

A man who didn't believe in keeping his love for his woman a secret. And he was protective. I liked that. I wanted that. Someone who'd scream from the mountain top, 'You're mine!'

"I'm here celebrating my birthday," I informed him.

"By yourself?" He sounded shocked. Almost as much as I was to be here alone. "Why on earth is a beautiful woman such as yourself celebrating her birthday alone?"

I sat up. "We're definitely going to need drinks if I'm going to answer that."

"I can get with that. Let me just tell the guys I'll be back in a few."

He stood up and started walking back towards his cabana. I sat up to collect my belongings since I wasn't sure if I'd be returning. Considering the chemistry I felt brewing between us, there was no telling where this night was headed. Though it wouldn't be in my bedroom for sure. My one time fantasy about having a one-night stand with a sexy stranger had been canceled, after catching too many episodes of Law and Order and Dateline on boring, date-less Friday nights.

I was in search of stability, romance...a forever love *with commitment*.

Once I'd collected everything, I grabbed my bag and eased off the lounge chair. By then, Tate was headed back towards me.

"Are you ready, Miss Ava?" he asked, cheesing from ear-to-ear.

"What's that look all about?"

He stared at me with a devilish grin that rivaled his smoldering gaze. There was something alluring yet frolicsome about him that I was drawn to. I'd dated enough serious guys in my lifetime to know I wanted someone who wasn't afraid to crack a joke. A great sense of humor was high up on my list of must-haves. We all had a little kid inside of us that sometimes needed to run free.

"Oh, so you aren't going to tell me?" I gave him a light, playful shove on his shoulder. "Fine, keep your secrets then."

He pulled me close to him, placing his hand in the crevice of my lower back as he moved his head closer to my ear. He'd granted me full access to his upper body, giving me ample time to smell the patchouli and blackcurrant notes permeating from his pores. Pretty sure he was wearing that irresistible Tom Ford cologne. I moaned internally at his touch on my flesh. His lips gently brushed against my earlobe as the warm breath trickling from his lips tickled my skin.

"I think we need to get to know each other a little better before I tell you what that look really means."

That was all I needed to get my imagination going.

This might not be a bad trip after all.

9

Chapter Nine: A Piece of Good Fortune

"Sttttooppppp," I said before bursting into laughter.

Tate and I had been talking, laughing, and drinking for the past three hours. I had completely lost track of time. Beneath his sexy, smoldering exterior was a comedian, and I hadn't laughed this hard in a long time. As the glasses piled up in front of us, I was reminded that I was on track for another night like the previous one.

Although, this one was different.

This time I had the company of a fine gentleman who triggered every sensory nerve in my body. I had hoped the tequila would help settle my nerves, or wrangle this pulsating sensation of excitement, maybe even calm these wild thoughts, but it didn't. All it did was push my sober thoughts to the back of my mind and make room for my caged inhibitions to run free.

"I'm serious, it really happened," he insisted. He rubbed his hand over his smooth bald head. "I ended up dancing on the bar in Tulum on video with a bottle in my hand in front of everyone. I was so drunk I didn't even realize I had stripped down to my trunks."

I couldn't stop laughing at him. The thought of him dancing on a bar alone had me dying. I'd always heard of women doing it. Rarely had I heard of men doing it. He didn't seem like the type. Tate gave me 'reserved guy off in the corner watching from afar' vibes. We'd been sharing crazy stories, but this was by far the funniest.

He grinned. "So now it's your turn. Tell me something outrageous you've done."

I took the last swig of my mango margarita.

"I promise I don't have anything as wild and crazy as that."

He tilted his head, looking at me with disbelief, turning up his lip. I knew it sounded far-fetched, but it was true. I had a few wild moments in college, but nothing too crazy. Nothing YouTube or Worldstar worthy. And it was mainly due to my mother insisting that I always must conduct myself in a respectable manner. She had zero tolerance for being embarrassed by her kids in public.

I shook my head. "I hate to break it to you, Tate, but I don't have anything nearly as crazy as that. There were a few typical college moments, that's it."

He smiled at me invitingly, "Well it's never too late."

I raised my eyebrow.

"For what?"

"To have a few wild memories. You are in Mexico. What happens on vacation, stays on vacation." He winked and grinned, inviting me with his eyes to partake in something unexpected.

"And I take it you want to be a part of those wild memories?"

He smirked. "I meeannnnn." His mischievous shrug prompted me to laugh.

"Nice try, mister, but it's not happening."

"If you say so. We'll see by the time you leave. How long are you here for again?"

I was reluctant to tell him. My vacation was pretty open at this point. The plans I originally laid out had completely changed. This was perhaps the first time in my whole life that I didn't have a well-thought-out itinerary. And surprisingly, it felt good. Great, even. Still, I wasn't quite sure I wanted to fill all of my birthday vacation time with him. Too much time with him could lead to other things.

Naughty things.

And I wasn't sure if that's where I saw this going.

"I'm here for eight days," I confided in him. "Though I may cut it shorter."

He asked, "Why would you do a silly thing like that? This is practically paradise."

I paused. We'd finally circled back to why I was here in this beautiful place, alone. I'd hoped we would avoid it, but he was going to pull it out of me. One way or another. What was crazy is that I actually felt comfortable telling him.

"I hadn't planned on being here alone," I answered solemnly.

"Then why are you?"

I inhaled deeply. "My friends decided not to come."

"Wow, that's..." He stared at me. "That's disappointing."

"Yeah, it is. But I guess it's partially my fault." I signaled the bartender for another drink. This conversation was going to have me in my feelings and alcohol seemed like the best coping mechanism right now. *And him,* I thought, allowing the smile that sat at the corner of my lip to stretch across my face then disappear. "I let my expectations get the best of me, and well, here I am."

He leaned back in his chair, readying himself for the story behind the saga of my friendships. The bartender slid my drink in front of me and I sipped it, hoping it would calm my thoughts that were competing with my rationale.

"Expectations aren't bad," he said.

I scoffed beneath my breath. "They are when you already know the outcome."

"Then why plan a trip of this magnitude if you knew they weren't coming?"

"I'm a glass half-full kind of gal. And I guess wishing got the best of me." I shrugged. "Although a part of me, a large part, knew it was going to end like this. I mean, yeah of course, I wish they had told me they weren't coming. But then again, here I am." I smiled a coy, but albeit defensive smile. It was hard to admit defeat to a perfect stranger. But the fact that he was, so far, quite perfect on the surface, made it that much easier to risk my feelings.

Maybe when it was all said and done, I would not care if they told me or not, if they even showed up for me or not, because maybe I would be glad to be in the dark. How else would I have found time alone with this gorgeous man right here, who has made more time for me today than any of them have in years. Perspective, Ava. I had to cheer myself on.

I fought to hide the sadness I felt brewing beneath the surface. This was why I didn't want to talk about this. I didn't want to rehash the feelings I'd already stuffed to the bottom of my soul. But maybe I did need to talk about it, get it out of my system once and for all, perhaps with someone who had an unbiased opinion. Maybe there was something I was missing.

"There's nothing wrong with hope or hoping for the best." Tate placed his hand over mine, reassuringly.

I asked, "Even when you're setting yourself up for disappointment?"

"You shot your shot," he said casually. "And sure, it didn't end the way you wanted it to, but at least you know. Moving forward, you have to make a decision on how to proceed. People always show you who they are, how you react to that revelation is completely up to you."

His optimism and cheery attitude were slowly becoming an aphrodisiac. I rested the rim of the glass against my lips, sipping slowly, contemplating what he said. He'd made several solid points and regardless of whether he knew the intimate details, his point was valid. I'd been pushing to reunite with my friends, took matters into my own hands, and really hadn't taken into account what they wanted. Had they even missed *me*?

But that was the point, wasn't it, to understand.

"You're right," I told him.

"Why didn't they come? If you don't mind me asking."

"Years of unresolved issues," I said matter-of-factly.

"And you hoped this trip would be a way to reconcile those issues," he stated, finishing my reply.

"You could say that. Since it was a major birthday for me, I figured we could attempt to set aside our differences long enough to rekindle our friendship. We were really close at one point, extremely close, but life and drama pulled us in opposite directions. Still, they weren't just my friends, they were like my sisters, and I miss them terribly."

"Life does that sometimes. The very people we thought would be around forever, through some twist of fate, leave us. But life also gives you new people, if you allow them in."

It certainly does. I smiled at his reference to himself.

"I agree."

"When is your birthday, Ava?"

"Tomorrow. Actually—" I glanced down at my wrist "—It's in an hour."

We chatted about many things until the lights got dim. With the exception of a few stragglers, the bar cleared out. There were a few people still dancing and socializing near the bar like we were. Between the songs and laughter, Tate and I shared occasional glances that bordered on flirty and suggestive. The nonchalant way he playfully touched me when we laughed had my skin standing at attention. I tried deciphering his intentions. Was it just the alcohol, or did he intentionally take his flirting to the next level, but at this point, it really

73

didn't matter. The brushes against my bare skin were every bit as inviting as his aura.

The DJ switched from the upbeat tunes he'd been playing to a more R&B vibe as we started finishing up the last of our drinks.

"Uh oh, you know what that means," Tate suggested.

I giggled at what he was alluding to. We both knew what the change in music meant. In just about every club, at least the ones we partied in, the DJ switching to slow jams indicated it was time to close.

"Yep, I do. Guess the night is over," I answered.

A devilish grin appeared on his lip. "We ain't got to go home."

And without missing a beat, I flashed him a big grin and finished the phrase, "but we can't stay here."

"Hmm, then where to next?"

I draped my arm over the back of the chair. The mischief splashed across his face had me wondering what he was up to. He took in the last of his mezcal in one sip, and slid out of his chair. Gazing up at him, I couldn't help but smile. The marvelous work God had done on him had not gone unnoticed. Every single inch that made up the six-two he was blessed with was placed perfectly.

He held his hand out. I glanced down at it then back up at him, raising an eyebrow in suspense.

"Miss Ava, will you dance with me? I'd love the honor of having your first dance for your..." he stopped as he waited for me to finish.

"I know your mother told you never to ask a woman her age." I shook my finger at him. "That is just rude." I smirked at him.

He placed his hand on his chest, pretending to be shocked. His subtle reaction caused me to laugh. His lightheartedness was refreshing.

"I mean my intention was never to offend, but as beautiful as you are, I'm sure your age is nowhere near a reflection of it."

He had me grinning from ear to ear. His charisma. His energy. His entire vibe, all of it was so damn intoxicating. How come men like him weren't in Los Angeles? I wondered. He would be a good candidate to entertain romantically. If this actually went anywhere, well, I know my mother would certainly approve. I would probably have to restrain Jade from throwing a parade or block party to celebrate the union.

I smiled at his attempt to pry my age out of me.

"To answer your question, I will be turning forty tomorrow."

His eyes widened as his mouth hung partially agape. He looked like Jim Carey on *The Mask* when he saw Cameron Diaz for the first time. It was hilarious, but not at all surprising. An internal fountain of youth was just one beauty secret black women possessed with little to no effort. Or as our ancestors and the billion-dollar cosmetics industry would call it—melanin. Melanin was black gold. Beautiful. Magical. Pure. It came in a variety of shades, each one just as remarkable as the next.

"Amazing," was the only word he uttered.

Our eyes connected and I felt like he was undressing me with his eyes, piercing through my soul, unraveling me thread-by-thread. The latter part he had no knowledge of, yet and still, he was the orchestrator of my emotions in this moment. I swallowed hard, trying to wrangle the temptress clawing her way to the surface.

I blushed. "Thank you."

Another moment of brief intense silence passed between. Our gazes remained locked as he waited for me to respond to his initial request. I inhaled slow, deep, feverish breaths. Glancing back down at his hand, I placed my hand inside of his palm. He helped me ease off the stool and guided me to the dance floor. Slow jam after slow jam, the DJ added to the ambiance and energy transmitting between us.

Tate pulled me close to him, and I rested my head on his muscular chest, breathing in his rousing masculine musk. His firm hand on the small of my back triggered a small gasp. I pursed my lips to exhale hoping it relieved the pressure below. Being this close to him, hearing his steady heartbeat, while his hand caressed the naked flesh on my back was electrifying.

The DJ played *A Sunday Kind of Love* and I felt like I was floating amongst the clouds. He tightened his grip around my waist, and I pressed my body closer to him. A natural cause and effect I hadn't experienced or wanted to experience in too many years. We swayed to the melody. I closed my eyes to take it all in. The sound of the waves became amplified, grounding me and reminding me to take it all in. I felt a sense of peace wash over me, as I reminded myself that this is what should naturally occur between a man and woman, in paradise.

No fighting on vacation, no cold silence in the airport lounge, no non-stop calls back to the office.

It was this type of peaceful companionship that I had been craving.

This moment required me to be fully present.

The tender way he held me emboldened me. My arms soon found their way around his neck. I stared into his dark brown eyes that gleamed. There was something in them. My reflection. The way I saw myself in them shook something inside of me. Happiness. Wonder. It felt good. Wholesome. And I wanted more of it.

He pulled his arm to look at his watch then placed his arm back around my waist.

"Happy Birthday, Ava."

10

Chapter Ten: Sunrises, Sea Breezes, and Surprises

Another morning, a new chapter, another sunrise. I stayed up to catch today's splendid display of nature, happy to enjoy it on my birthday. Sitting in reverence of how the sky had been painted with a new canvas, I admired how it was nothing like the morning before, yet just as beautiful. The cotton candy skies perched above me looked as if a pack of Starburst had exploded across the horizon. Shades of light and dark pinks converged effortlessly with oranges, yellows, and reds, creating a stunning effect.

As daybreak emerged, the sun crept above the horizon, dismissing the starry sky I danced beneath last night. A grateful smile formed on my lips, and I thanked the universe for another opportunity to live out my purpose. The peace and tranquility of ringing in my fortieth birthday with a perfect stranger who seemed honestly perfect for me, well, that gave me a chance to really take in how far I'd come in life, how great my life turned out, and despite the fact that I had lost some things and people along the way, I was still surrounded by love. Life had indeed treated me well.

My mother called an hour ago. She hadn't expected me to answer since it was so early, but I hadn't yet gone to sleep. I was still floating on a high from my night with Tate. I didn't tell her that, so I pretended to yawn, and thanked her for calling me.

We had the talk we usually had on my birthday and on Christmas morning. Expressions of gratitude flowing both ways. Although she was tough on me, my Mom was always reminding me of how much she loved being my mother. I took this day to express to her genuinely how much she meant to me, and we were both shedding tears by the end of the call. If anything was left unsaid, then we will cover it again on Christmas Eve, with me being sentimental and softened up by her famous homemade sweet potato pie and oatmeal chocolate chip cookies.

Jade texted a few hours before because ever since we were kids, we liked being the first to wish each other happy birthday.

I closed my eyes and dug my fingers into the grainy sand, breathing in the tiny hints of salt in the sea breeze. I really needed to do more of this. Go to the beach and just unwind. We had plenty of them back home, and I pledged to myself that I was going to start enjoying them a lot more often, as part of my new self care routine.

The wind blew through the loose strands of hair not constricted in the messy bun I brushed my hair up in. I couldn't remember the last time I felt so at peace. I spent most of my twenties and all of my thirties grinding and working hard. Rarely did I stop to relax. There was always a new project to launch, that business to expand, or this bag to secure. All of it became so time consuming, that I rarely had time to devote to myself. Until I opened my affirmation journal and sat down to write, from the heart, it truly never dawned on me how much of my social life I sacrificed.

Especially love.

My cheeks rose thinking about Tate. The way he made me feel, the butterflies I tried to keep at bay, his general disposition—I liked it. And I wanted to be around more of it. The only issue was we were just two strangers on vacation. Once we left here, it was back to reality.

Doubt formed in my mind.

Followed by thoughts of me wasting my time, which began to take over.

Live in the moment, Ava.

I shook off the self-sabotage that started to creep up. This didn't need to happen. There was no point in giving negative energy to a situation that didn't require it. Standing to my feet, I dusted the sand off of me and turned to walk back to my room.

Tate had asked me to breakfast after walking me back to my villa and I agreed. I was going to enjoy his company for as long as I was able to. Why not?

The sand was starting to warm up as the sun got higher in the sky. As I drew closer to my villa, I saw shadows of silhouettes. I stopped dead in my tracks. My breath got caught in my throat while the rest of my body stood paralyzed in one spot.

"Who the hell is in my villa?" I mumbled.

It was too early for room service, which I hadn't even ordered, so I knew it wasn't that. Besides, I had enough towels and clean sheets— thanks to no one showing up- so I didn't need any of those. I regained my senses and started moving quickly towards my villa. Security was pretty tight around here, but this was still concerning. Whoever the hell thought it was a good idea to break into my room was going to be in for a rude awakening.

I'd heard stories and even read reviews of tourists' rooms getting broken into while on vacation, but I never imagined I'd be one of them. My thoughts became chaotic—going from one extreme to the next— trying to figure out what my next move should be, to stay safe.

Ava, what are you going to do if it's a burglar?

I looked around to see if there was something solid and heavy that I could pick up to hit whoever was in my villa, take them out with a clean shot. I found a thick branch and picked it up. Best case scenario, I'd incapacitate them long enough for the authorities to arrive. Worst case scenario, they'd incapacitate me.

I ran up the hill, slightly out of breath, finally making it to the front door. My eyes bulged when I saw there were several people inside of my house. A few of them had cameras. Others had video equipment, handheld lights, and large black cords were stretched across the hall and the main room of the villa. Everyone was moving about like it was okay for them to be here.

"What the hell!" I blurted out, busting through my door. "Who the hell are you all and what are you doing in my damn villa?" I was not using my indoor voice. Not today.

Heads abruptly turned in my direction as everyone froze. Confusion was plastered on their faces indicating they were unsure how to respond. Or if they should. I placed one hand on my hip, gripping the branch with the other, waiting for someone to say something before I called the police. Is it still 9-1-1 in Mexico? Well, damn.

I rolled my neck. "I know somebody better say something or every last one of y'all are going to jail today!" Eyes roamed back-and-forth as they all waited for someone to speak up. "Hey! Who's in charge?"

A chubby man stepped out front with a black t-shirt with the word *Director* in white block lettering across his chest. He looked unsure of whether he should answer or not. A highly irritated woman was standing in front of him with a branch ready to go berserk on him and his crew, so that would be good cause for concern.

I motioned for him to speak. And now.

"Good morning, ma'am, my name is Ian Smith. I'm the executive producer of the show *Evergreen Family Values*. We were told we had permission to be here," he replied. The uncertainty in his voice led me to believe he wasn't as sure as he appeared to be. "We're here on behalf of Brave Girl Productions."

"Of what and who?"

"We're the producers of Evergreen Family Values...it's a reality television show. Olivia Evergreen is the main star of the show," he added, while giving me a bit of side eye. He was short, burly and cocky, and used a tone as if I should already know these things.

My brow furrowed at the mention of Olivia's name. And a damn reality tv show. I hated reality tv shows, it was cringey to watch people exploit themselves and expose their deepest secrets for a check. There had to be a better way for Olivia to secure her bag. Wow.

Not only had Olivia shown up two days late, completely out of the blue, with not a single call or text, she was here with a damn film crew. I took a deep breath to calm the slow brewing anger I felt rising to the surface. The response I wanted to give shouldn't be directed towards him. He was only adhering to what he'd been told. I softened my expression enough to give him a modest grin. For a brief moment, I actually saw the humor in this ridiculousness.

"Where is Olivia?" I asked.

He pointed up. "I believe she's walking one of my intern camera guys around so he can get some B-roll footage of the villa."

My eyes widened in fury. *She knows she's out of pocket for this.* There were a ton of lines she had crossed, mostly personal ones, but legal lines as well. I knew that a production like this required waivers and all kinds of permissions before filming commenced. Not to mention, she hadn't even asked *me* if I wanted to be on this "Surprise!" reality tv show.

Folding my arms across my chest, I tapped my foot against the tile. It was the only reaction I could muster up that didn't result in me using every expletive I could think of. I contemplated what I wanted to do about this invasion. Did I want to gather her in front of everyone or did

I want to storm up the stairs and give her a piece of my mind? Either way the whole house was going to hear what I had to say.

I chose the latter and eased towards the stairs. My hand touched the railing and I paused to look back towards the group of people standing completely still, waiting for what wrath was to come.

I decided to take both the stairs and the high road, and speak to the camera crew with some measure of respect. Most importantly, I did not want to find myself looking like a fool on national television just because Olivia had agreed to do so.

"If you all don't mind, please wait outside for a moment until I sort this out. I haven't given anyone permission to film me or to film inside of my residence," I made it crystal clear with my pointed tone and the sharpness of my pronunciation of each and every syllable. What was implied was 'lawsuit incoming, standby.'

I looked at their shocked faces, and saw that my threat had landed. "It should just be a few moments, then I'll send Olivia out to let you know how you may proceed." And by that I actually meant, grab your crap and be gone.

Ian nodded and gave the order for everyone to wait outside. I gave them a sarcastic half-smile as I waited for them to pack their equipment up and leave. Once everyone had exited, I proceeded upstairs to check Olivia about her brazen intrusiveness. My foot hit the top step and I caught a glimpse of her in the bedroom speaking into the camera. Normally, I would be polite and wait, but since she failed to show me the same courtesy, she'd have to deal with whatever came her way.

"Olivia!" I yelled from the hallway. "What the hell is going on?"

She jerked her head to the side and saw the furiousness that covered my face. The cameraman spun around to get a glimpse of my face too.

"Get that freakin' camera out of my face," I told him. "Olivia, are you serious right now? Who the hell are these people? And why are they filming in the villa I paid for?"

Olivia rushed past him, embarrassment flooding her face, as she beckoned for me to calm down. "Ava, pleeease," she pleaded, "Please calm down."

"What?" I genuinely could not fathom someone behaving this way. For the last ten years I have built a solid media business based on accountability, following through, following the rules of my industry until I reached the top. That works. What was this stupidity?

I shifted my weight to my right hip and placed my hand on top of it. The audacity of her asking me to calm down when she just pulled this stunt was crazy.

"You have a lot of nerve asking me to calm down when you show up here with a film crew, no heads up or anything. I called you several times to see what happened and if you were even coming and you never responded. That's really jacked up, Olivia!" Now, seeing her face to face, weirdly brought me right back to the lingo of our college days.

"I thought you'd be happy to see me," she said with a perplexed look on her face. "I didn't call because I wanted to surprise you." She gave wide eyes and innocent face.

"Or because you knew you were coming with an entire film crew?" I questioned her motives openly.

She rolled her eyes.

"You always find the negative in things, don't you?" Her smart aleck response caught me off guard. This was not the response I expected. At the very least I figured she'd apologize for her little stunt, but nope, not Olivia. Why was I not surprised?

I rubbed the agitation out of my temple.

"If you think you're going to flip this around on me, you have another thing coming. You and I both know your little 'surprise'—" I air quoted "—was because you knew I would say *hell no* to a film crew being here. Let's not make it about *me* when this is really about *you*."

Her jaw dropped. She pretended to be offended but it was pointless.

We both knew the truth, which was this was a *typical* Olivia antic. Knowing her, she'd spent the last two weeks planning this. Making travel arrangements for an entire crew took time. Hence her late arrival.

"Why can't you just go with the flow for once?" she snapped back.

"Excuse me?"

She doubled down on her stance. "I mean seriously, Ava. You've always been so stuffy. Loosen up a bit. You don't have to control *everything,* all the time. This could be a good thing for you as well. Maybe people will get to see the cool, lighter side of you."

Did she...I know she didn't just say that.

"I beg your pardon?" I raised an eyebrow. "Are you really attempting to call me out when you're in the wrong?"

She sighed heavily.

"I mean, did I say something untrue?"

"That's not the point, Olivia. You brought a slew of people on a vacation I invited you on and paid for. If you were going to do this, why didn't your little tv show pay for your travel?"

"So this is about the money? My 'little' tv show? Girl, what?" Olivia stared at me coldly and looked rather hurt, to be honest.

"Really? You know it's not. It's about your failure to communicate with me."

"So are you saying they can't be here?"

I snickered mockingly. Her ability to manipulate a situation was still ever present. Guilt-tripping too. Olivia was going to put the ball in my court so if it went left, it would be on me instead of her.

I asked, "What do you think?" Now we were at the standoff point, a question for a question, this was so typical of our old ways.

"Ava, please, I need this to happen," she said softly.

Her expressions shifted. This time displaying more humility than cockiness. While she stood here throwing jabs, she knew at the end of the day, she needed me to sign off on this; otherwise, it was a wrap—

literally.

"And what is this?" I inquired, wanting to know what crazy get-rich idea she was chasing this time. Olivia had always been a wanderer, a free-spirit, who floated wherever the wind blew her. She was gutsy and whatever genius idea she had at the moment, she went with it. There wasn't anything wrong with that, except for the fact that she *never* stuck with anything. She was a great visionary, but not so great with the execution. Now she was doing a reality tv show and it screamed *trendy* and *for the moment*, which worried me. And reminded me of why we'd fallen out in the first place.

But I digressed.

I inhaled, softening my demeanor. I was happy to see her, that much was true, my issue was I wished she'd gone about this differently. We were too old and experienced in life now, for the 'ask for forgiveness, instead of permission' approach.

"Liv, you know I will always support you. But I don't like being ambushed and we both know that's what you did! You could've easily sent me a text or email asking me if I was cool with this. I have a business, a reputation among my clients, to consider. It's both professional and personal... this wasn't the way to handle this," I chastised her.

She pressed her palms against the other as she clenched her teeth together. The high and mighty attitude had suddenly become her pleading with me to allow this.

"You're right, but I meant what I said. This could be good for your image as well," she reiterated.

"I don't need an image overhaul, Olivia. Neither does my brand. I don't want my personal business splashed all over television and the internet," I reminded her, still deliberating whether I wanted to allow this or not. Until meeting Tate, I didn't have that much personal business to speak of in the first place, if I were being transparent.

I gazed at her. "However, I can see this is something you're passion-ate about." *For now,* I thought. "With that being said, your film crew can stay as long as *you* agree they will film you and only you. I do not want to and I will not be in any of the footage."

Her face sunk and she stared at me, clueless.

"Ava, what are they going to film then? It's just me and you here." Well, that didn't sting at all. Thanks, Olivia.

"Look, they can film you at the beach in a bikini I suppose, I don't know. Ask your producer, Ian. But these are my terms. Take them or leave them," I emphasized my stubbornness by putting my hands on my hips and tilting up my chin, like I was taking a cover photo for Forbes magazine.

Olivia hesitated. The cameraman appeared stunned waiting for her answer. She sighed then dropped her shoulders. "What if we adjust the terms a teeny bit..." She pinched her fingers together. "And let's say they don't film anything personal, including conversations, crazy moments, etcetera."

I closed my eyes, and huffed. I had to admit, the idea of becoming slightly more well known might not be the worst thing for my brand. If I were able to have some creative control, and never be shown in a bad light, maybe a little P.R. wouldn't be so bad. Since BLM, companies have been scrambling to hire black owned businesses, and I could always use more clients, that's always the goal.

"Fine, Olivia." I gave her a serious glare. " Under no circumstances does anything personal get filmed. I mean it. If I see anything that remotely resembles something personal, I will sue the entire network and have a cease-and-desist served. Do I make myself clear?"

Olivia nodded gleefully. Then she ran towards me and wrapped her arms around me, squeezing me tightly.

"Thank you, Ava. You won't regret this," she assured me.

I patted her arm. "I hope not."

"You won't, I promise." Her embrace tightened. "Oh and happy birthday, old lady!"

11

Chapter Eleven: Spill the Beans

This started out as a hectic morning thanks to Olivia's impromptu arrival. And thanks to that foolishness, my breakfast date with Tate was postponed on account of an entire production team accompanying her. I texted him shortly after agreeing to let the film crew stay, explaining to him what occurred, then requested a rain check. The last thing I wanted was for his privacy to be invaded on account of my friend. He seemed to be sad at first, even a bit distant, but then he happily rescheduled for lunch instead. I promised him I would do my best to carve out some time later on today to see him.

Hopefully, Olivia needed to get some footage for her show, so I could sneak off with him. I knew it would end up being just a quick lunch, since Olivia was my guest and she was finally here, but I couldn't pass up the opportunity to see Tate again.

I glanced at myself in the mirror, and noticed a fresh glow. If this was forty, I'll take it. My skin looked sun-kissed and blemish free. My hair had taken on some cute sea-salt air waviness and bounce. There was definitely a fresh sparkle of excitement in my eye.

I beamed at my forty year old self,and thought, 'Ava 4.0, you are the upgrade! I approve.' I'm watching the inward smile rise to the surface of my lips. I feel like a blushing bride as thoughts of Tate seeing me, all glowed up danced across my mind.

I swiped a generous pat of Fenty lip gloss across my puckered lips trying to remember the last time I felt this giddy inside. Popping my lips, I made sure I had evenly distributed the gloss on them then moved my head side-to-side to check out my profile. Mentally approving of my day look, I finger-combed through my hair. Since I'd been here, I had worn it up in a bun. Today, I was going for a relaxed, softer look-let the curls be free to do what they do.

"Ava, are you ready?" Olivia yelled down the hall. She used to be cheer captain, so her voice traveled like no other.

She'd been here less than six hours and already there was an influx of noise. It dawned on me after she'd been here an hour, the peace and quiet of my first day on my own wasn't so bad. Tugging on the knot I tied in my bandeau top, I made sure it was tight enough to withhold this chest no matter what drama ensued. The last thing I wanted was for one of her cameramen to catch my boobs falling out. I'd be devastated.

"Yes, almost. I'll be in out a few," I answered, spinning around in the floor length mirror. Prior to my trip, I purchased a few new outfits. All of them were light, airy, and loose fitting like the ensemble I had on. The wide leg pants provided the right amount of space and room for air to flow freely through them. On my feet were a pair of bling bedazzled slides. My Aquazurra heels were reserved for evening events only. I fixed the large, gold hoops in my ear then winked at myself. My look was giving true island princess, like Rihanna herself would be proud, and I was finally starting to feel relaxed here.

"Oooh, you look cute, girl," Olivia shouted in my direction. "I like that outfit. Where did you get that from?"

I answered, "Fashion Nova."

She raised her eyebrow curiously.

"You shop at Fashion Nova?"

I detected a hint of surprise in her tone. Though I didn't know why. Lots of women shopped at Fashion Nova. It was cute, trendy and the bonus was it was inexpensive, and designed for a shapely body. I shopped everywhere to be honest. I liked variety. My closet was full of couture, name brands, and also pieces from Fashion Nova or small boutiques. I never considered myself above shopping in various places, and had no problem popping into a TJ Maxx or grabbing a swimsuit at Target. Who cares?

"Don't sound so surprised," I teased.

"I'm just saying. I wouldn't think someone like you would shop at Fashion Nova."

I furrowed my brow. "Someone like me?"

"You know what I'm saying, Ava..." She placed her hand on her hip. "We all know you're filthy rich. I thought you'd only be shopping at Neiman Marcus or someplace like that."

"I do, but I like stuff from Fashion Nova, too," I said, correcting her pre-judgement of me. "I mix-and-match pieces all the time. To me, it's not about labels, it's about what I like. If I find a cute vintage piece at a market, let me try it on."

She waved her hand, snapping her fingers.

"Okay, sis. I hear you. But you're on your own with the thrifting. I don't wear second hand clothing. No ma'am, you don't know where that came from, or what energy it holds. Hmm, no."

I examined her attire, noticing she was in head-to-toe labels. Her sandals, pants, purse, and sunglasses had Fendi monograms splashed all over them. *Reality television obviously paid well.* The only thing without a monogram was her white crop top. And I wouldn't have been surprised if it was labeled too. Olivia embodied the reality tv chick persona in its entirety. Super long fake nails, stacks of gold bangles, and 'extra' attitude for days. I prayed I wasn't going to end up strangling her for doing something extremely ratchet that got on my nerves.

"I can see." I waved my finger up and down. "Girl, you're dripping in designer."

"Only the best for these curves of mine."

She spun around showing off her sculpted body. I didn't want to assume she had work done. That was stereotypical, but unfortunately not so far-fetched. Most of the women on those shows had some kind of work done to keep up appearances—and ensure that those checks kept rolling in. And most times, they simply took it too far.

"Can you believe we're forty though? Liv, you look great!" I complimented her. I might inquire later about a recommendation for a surgeon, who knows?

My anti-cosmetic surgery stance had weakened considerably after my thirty ninth birthday, and here we are today looking square in the face of the big four-o. But I am so grateful to have made it here, that's the thing. I am truly grateful because aging is a privilege and a gift.

She flipped her hair confidently. "Results from 5 a.m. workouts and eating clean. I can give you my trainer's info if you want."

My face scrunched up. Should I be offended? Liv always had a funny way of 'helping a sister out', that could feel like a backhand slap in the face.

"Nah, girl, I don't mean it like that. You look great, are you kidding me?" Olivia held her hands up. "I'm just saying, Beast can get you all the way together though. He's the best."

She cleaned that up quickly, I thought. A smirk sat at the corner of my mouth.

"Come on, girl." I wasn't going to respond to her slight shade. Especially since I wasn't buying the *workout only* story she was selling me. "Let's go eat. I'm starving."

* * *

I stared at my phone, somewhat upset.

"What's wrong?" Olivia asked, stuffing an almond and cream cheese Danish into her mouth. "You look like you've seen a ghost, what is going on?"

I looked at her. "My lunch date that was supposed to be a breakfast date got canceled." Honestly, I felt as crushed as the crumbs at the bottom of a bag of potato chips.

Tate had texted that he had a work emergency and would need to catch up later on tonight. I was moderately disappointed, but I understood. There'd been plenty of times that I was *supposed* to be on vacation, when in reality I ended up working.

Her eyes widened as she chewed, slowly deflating her round cheeks. I could tell she was trying to figure out who I was supposed to be meeting for lunch.

"A lunch date?" she asked inquisitively. "You met someone here already?"

I sipped my coffee. The hazelnut flavor went down smoothly as I nodded in response to her question. "Yes, the other day matter of fact."

"Okay, Stella. Someone moves quickly," she teased. "Guess you came here looking for your Winston."

I laughed behind my mug trying to hide that I was blushing. Her correlation to me and Terry McMillan's fictional character was humorous and partially befitting.

"I wouldn't say all of that. We met and hung out. Then he asked me to join him for breakfast since it was my birthday and he knew I was here alone."

"I see. Well, what does this mysterious man look like? And where is he? I want to see him. What does he do? Can he keep up with you, or what?"

Her series of questions flew out quicker than I had time to process them, and with a partial mouth full of food at that. Olivia stared at me as she waited for me to respond. I almost did until I caught a glimpse of someone from the camera crew lurking a few feet from us. *This is exactly why I should've said no.* Sighing inwardly, I looked back at her. I hated that I had to mince my words, but I was adamant about my personal business being exempt from this show.

"He's nice looking," was all I said before taking another sip.

"Annnddddd??" she asked, leaning back in her chair. "I'm waiting. I inquired about a few things, so let's hear it."

I set my mug down.

"You know what, let's save that for later. I want to hear about you. What have you been up to?" I cleverly dodged.

She side-eyed me. "Mm hmm, you ain't slick, Ava. I'll be circling back around to your mystery man, but we can put a pin in that topic for now. Anyhow, I've been cool."

I noticed a gradual shift in her tone as she vaguely answered my question. Cool wasn't the response I was expecting considering we were on vacation being followed around by a production crew. At the very least, I thought she'd jump at the opportunity to tell me she was famous now. Olivia wasn't known for her modesty.

"That's all...just cool?" I questioned.

"What do you mean?"

"Look around, Liv," I signaled. "You came with a film crew for heaven's sake."

She shrugged her shoulders nonchalantly. Brushing off my attempt to recognize her success. Almost as if starring on a tv show was an everyday occurrence.

"Yeah, I mean it's just a reality tv show, though. Nothing close to a sitcom or anything."

She's still doing it, I thought, shaking my head.

She was dumbing down her lifestyle which was odd considering she was sitting across from me, decked out in designer attire. I was expecting specifics, some bragging even, definitely not dismissal. Then again, Olivia always did struggle with confidence. Even when we were younger, she would get compliments and blow them off. Or shrink. Or do the most to hide her insecurities.

She wrestled with seeing herself like others saw her.

Hence her inability to commit to anything for long periods of time. She never thought she was good enough. And it was a shame because most people would love to have a free-spirit like hers. I didn't have an envious bone in my body, but I wished I could throw caution to the wind like she did at times and just live in the moment.

"Is there something I'm missing?" I inquired. "I don't know what it actually takes to secure a television show, or even a reality show, but I would assume it's not easy. Give yourself some credit, Liv."

I watched her shoulders droop a bit.

Her lackadaisical demeanor indicated something else was going on.

"Olivia." I leaned in and remembered how we used to sit and talk for hours over coffee back in the day. "Hey, is everything OK?"

"It's fine." Her response was dismissive, once again. "Nothing I can't handle."

I picked up my mug and took another sip. There was definitely something she wasn't telling me. Something I couldn't quite put my finger on but knew she was hiding. She'd eventually tell me. We were here for six more days. The truth would inevitably come out sooner or later, right?

12

Chapter Twelve: The Diva Has Arrived

After our mid-morning coffee and conversation, Olivia and I walked along the beach. I wanted her to enjoy the serene scenery that I'd been able to enjoy these past two days. The first part of the walk was super quiet and a bit awkward. I wasn't sure if it stemmed from how our conversation ended, or whether it was due to the fact that we had barely spoken in close to seven years. Olivia was the last person in our friend group that I'd lost contact with, so it was even weirder than I had anticipated to be in the same space again.

And strangely, her exit from my life hurt the most.

Probably because a huge part of me felt like she used me and then when she knew she needed to pay me back—she ghosted me instead. That entire scenario left me feeling as though our friendship had been based on convenience rather than real, genuine friendship. Ironically, at the time, I never cared about the money, or if she was ever able to pay me back.

She was my friend, she needed my help, so I helped her. She had a big dream and I wanted to help her achieve it. We were in our twenties, all dreamers, and if your friends didn't believe in you, then who would?

Did I know at the time that it was another one of her fly by night moments? Yes. Was I completely aware of the fact that I'd probably never see that money again? Of course. Still, none of that mattered. What mattered was her being honest and forthcoming. Not treating me like her personal financier whenever she got a brilliant idea that she needed funded.

"You're pretty quiet, Ava. What's going through your mind?" she asked me.

I grinned. "Nothing," I lied. "Just taking in the scenery."

Really, Ava!

"Seems like you're deep in thought over there," she added.

I wondered if she noticed that because she was doing the same. I knew we hadn't talked in a few years, but I was still able to discern when something was off with her. But I digressed. Today wasn't the day I was going to force anyone to share their feelings. It was *my* birthday and I wanted as much peace and joy as possible.

I glanced at the ocean. "I'm just thinking about what I want this next chapter of my life to look like."

She nodded silently. A partial grin touched her lips, which soon faded into a frown. Olivia was always awful at masking her feelings or hiding when something was wrong with her. I wanted to know what was bothering her, but part of me felt like I didn't have the right to ask. So much time had passed between us that I wondered if the space to be transparent still existed. I wondered whether she felt comfortable enough spilling her secrets and opening up her soul to someone who she once considered her sister.

"If there's something you want to talk about, I want you to know I'm here, Liv. No judgement. Simply listening," was all I told her as I reached over and slid my arm through her elbow, pulling her closer in. This was my way of letting her know I was here for her and despite everything, we were still friends. "This trip isn't just about me. It's about reconnecting and rebuilding what we all lost so many years ago."

She looked at me. "And what's that, Ava?"

We paused and I released her arm so that we could face each other. I sighed as I looked into her eyes, which were seemingly filled with doubt and possibly regret at having ventured out to Mexico in the first place.

Out of all of us, Olivia could've been a fashion supermodel, hell, an icon, but she fell in love with someone that loved pretty women and fast money, and his scammer, get-rich-quick mindset rubbed off on her. Oftentimes I wished I could give her some of my ambition to fuel the potential she already possessed. It hurt watching her squander her incredible potential, and it was especially painful to witness her waste time with a loser.

Not that my own choices had been perfect, as Cameron certainly was nobody's prize in the end. However, I couldn't understand why Olivia had this gaping blind spot.

"Our friendship...our sisterhood. I miss it, Olivia. I miss all of the girls," I admitted. "That feeling is why I invited all of you here. I didn't want to go another year without being surrounded by genuine relationships."

She searched my eyes for the sincerity I felt deep within. Then she smiled at me.

"I appreciate you saying that, I really do." She exhaled lightly. "And I want you to know that I have missed you too. But I promise you, I'm okay. I'm going to enjoy this vacation. Drama free. Let's celebrate your birthday, sis!"

I quirked an eyebrow.

"Are you sure? You seem like something is weighing on you."

She shook her head. "I promise, I'm good," she said, looking behind me at what I knew was probably the camera crew. Her apprehension to speak about what was bothering her made me question why she was doing this in the first place. "I'm trying to get used to this reality star life, that's all. It is a lot more than I bargained for, I can tell you that much. But I am okay. It's handled."

I giggled a bit at that, because we always used *'It's handled'* as a sign off from our days of watching Kerry kill it on *Scandal,* with our bowls of popcorn and bottles of red. Yes, bottles. There were four of us and we gathered religiously on Thursday nights for a catch up session, including free group therapy followed by a gossip fest.

I didn't believe her, when she assured me that she was fine, but I was going to leave well enough alone. For now anyway. The last thing I wanted to do was push her. She'd only shut down even further. And I didn't want to ruin the trip.

Olivia didn't make eye contact at all, but instead looked out at the waves pounding the shoreline. Cabo beaches were beautiful and dramatic, but unfortunately were not suitable for swimming. Look, but don't get in. The analogy wasn't lost on me, I had been operating just this way for years, *don't get too close to me.* I'm just admitting the damage Cameron had done, and the extent of repairs needed to my heart if I were going to be whole and ready to love.

"You don't have to worry about me, Ava." Olivia attempted to reassure me.

Red flag number one. And usually what people said when something was *very* wrong but they didn't want to talk about it.

"Okay," I answered softly, and conceded for the time being. "However, if there is anything you want to talk about, ever, I am serious about being willing to listen. Any time."

"I appreciate it." Her right hand tapped me quickly on my arm, like some kind of sweet older church lady getting your attention when it's time to pass on the plate. Her attention was somewhere else and it had me worried.

Olivia seemed to at least pick up on my hesitant vibes, and suddenly brought on her actress voice. "Ava, you're the birthday girl! Can we celebrate? Now, c'mon, let's get this day started! I want to see what this resort has to offer. I have never been to Cabo, show me around this beautiful resort."

I nodded, fully agreeing with her. Today should be at least partly about me, absolutely.

She intertwined our arms, turning us around to head to our villa. It reminded me of the early days on campus when we all would walk the quad, arms linked and our steps in unison. We were pioneering the 'personal brand' even before it became a thing on Instagram. Sometimes we coordinated outfits and hairstyles, just to make a point. We self-declared that we were *the* hot freshman chicks, here to takeover the place. I could only laugh at our eighteen year old selves' arrogance and our collective naiveté.

On our way I was trying to think of what we could do today that would be a happy medium between us enjoying this trip and Olivia getting the dramatic footage she needed to ensure the show's success. I was still not entirely comfortable, and still up in the air about them being here, but I was trying to be a good friend and support her dreams. Even if they were temporary or didn't pan out into a long career, it was what Olivia wanted, so why not try to help her. Again.

As we reached the property, I noticed a black SUV parked in front of the villa. The two of us stared at each other. "Olivia, who is that?"

She shrugged unknowingly. "I have no idea."

"Are you expecting someone?" I asked.

"No, I came with everyone I planned to come with," she said, staring back at the car in our driveway. "Your guess is as good as mine."

I started towards the villa. The camera crew followed closely behind us. My patience for unexpected people popping up was wearing thin. As I opened the door, and we walked in, I heard a familiar noise I immediately recognized. A cackling sound that was bougie, cringey, and humorous at the same time. I took a deep, frustrated breath as I came to the unfortunate conclusion that indeed no one felt the need to call ahead.

"I take it you know who's here," Olivia stated as we moved closer to the sound.

"You do too."

Her eyes expressed confusion, which surprised me. That was a voice that if you heard it once, you would never forget. Much as you might try.

"It's Camille! She made the trip." I finished her thoughts.

Looking over at her I saw her lips twitch. I wasn't sure if that was a good reaction or bad. I'd lost touch with all of them and hadn't been sure if they'd kept in touch. Olivia not recognizing Camille's over-the-top laugh led me to believe that they hadn't talked very much either in the last few years. We walked into the kitchen and saw she was on the phone. I held my finger to my lips so Olivia wouldn't say anything.

"You need to tell her, or I will," she whispered into her phone. "I don't want to hear it. You promised. No, you keep saying you're done, so be done. I'm sick of being in the dark. I deserve better than this. Either you handle it, or I'm done."

I stared at her.

Her conversation sparked my curiosity. And I wondered what she had gotten herself entangled in this time. By the sound of it, she was up to her usual antics.

Chasing behind somebody else's man.

"Ahem." Clearing my throat, I smirked at her. "Camille!"

She turned around, smiling from ear-to-ear, with her phone pressed to her ear. Like Olivia, she didn't look like she had aged at all. Camille was as glamorous as they came. The fresh braids she sported were long, brown, and crimson, giving her an African goddess look. Her makeup, though soft, was a full beat, and I was surprised considering I never remembered her liking makeup. However it complemented her cocoa brown skin beautifully. Instead of showing any signs of aging, she looked like she was ready to step onto somebody's stage, maybe an opening act for Beyonce's worldwide tour. Honestly, Camille had always been the undeniable diva of the group.

"Let me call you back, darling," she murmured to whoever she was speaking to. "My girls have arrived!"

I shifted my weight to my right side and crossed my arms. My fallout with Camille didn't hurt me as much as the other two, but it stung. Mainly because what she'd done would ultimately tarnish the group. Turns out we fell apart anyway.

So much for that, I thought, cracking a big smile. I was really happy that she made the effort and she showed up, even if a day late and a dollar short, she made it to Mexico.

Camille placed her phone down on the marble counter top and started moving towards us. Her arms were open, and she smiled widely. "Hey, y'all," she said gleefully.

I glanced over at Olivia. She looked puzzled, trying to calculate the timeline of how we were all suddenly reunited. After a few minutes, the bemused expression became a smile stretched across her lips.

"Millie, what are you doing here?" Olivia walked towards her and embraced her. "I didn't know you were coming."

"Hey, Liv, long time no see," she replied.

"Me either," I chimed in. "I thought you had a big event to plan."

At least that was the excuse she'd given me. Camille grinned at me over Olivia's shoulder before they separated.

"I moved some things around. Turning forty is a big deal, sis! Look, I figured, what the hell—I haven't had a vacation in a while."

I couldn't tell how my face was looking, but I knew how I felt on the inside. Emotionally I was torn. Her phone conversation that I had just overheard was unsettling. Flashing a friendly smile, I eased closer to her for a hug. Since forever, we always greeted like sisters, with hugs, no matter what might be going on under the surface.

Her reason for being here, whatever it was, didn't matter that much now. She made the effort, she was here. All of the other stuff would work itself out. After all, I called this mini-reunion for the sole purpose of working it all out, right?

We embraced tightly.

"It's good to see you, Millie," I told her. "It's been what...ten years now?"

She smirked. "Something like that and it's just Camille now." She gave a theater pause to emphasize that this wasn't negotiable. "I haven't gone by Millie in a long time, ages."

And there's the diva.

Olivia's face scrunched up. I laughed inside and possibly let out a small snort, knowing Camille not wanting to be called by her childhood nickname was mainly attached to this new persona she adopted once her business took off.

"Oh, you big stuff now so we can't call you the only name we've called you for years?" Olivia blurted out.

Camille tilted her head back, letting out a fake laugh. "Now, Liv, you know it's nothing like that. I just left a lot of old things in the past, including that nickname."

"Okay girl," Olivia casually waved at her, "We'll call you by your government name if that's what you really want."

I laughed at Olivia. Camille's request seemed to annoy her much more than it did me, but that wasn't anything new either. Camille playfully sneered at her. I sensed a little tension between them and wondered if...

"It's cool. I mean I'm always in 'brand' mode—" she gestured with her fingers "—and sometimes I forget I'm not at work."

I wanted to roll my eyes but refrained from doing so. Prior to getting here I was in a good mood, and I was going to remain in one. It was my birthday for heaven's sake. And I still had something exciting to look forward to: Tate.

"I'm gonna change real quick and I'll be ready to turn up, Ava," Olivia announced.

"Oh my goodness, how could I forget?" Camille exclaimed innocently, "Ava, darling...happy birthday!" She reached into her Louis Vuitton and handed me a small package, wrapped exquisitely in pink and gold, my favorite colors. That was a thoughtful touch.

She eased closer to embrace me again. I softly patted her on the back, smiling at her willingness to *finally* show up, with gift in hand, after all of these years. "Thank you, Camille." I stepped back. "And thank you for coming. It means a lot."

"No thanks required. We're friends," she replied. "And I know I'm three days late, but you know how it is—the life of an entrepreneur."

I arched an eyebrow at her grasping attempt to find the common ground in our current lives. Camille and I fell out not too long after Lauren stopped speaking to me. The disbandment of our friendship was more on her behalf than mine, and for reasons she didn't want to come forth with. That being said, her being here now had me stumped. I definitely invited her, but I was leery about doing so, and this late entrance and her diva attitude just reinforced my doubts.

Jade was in my head, saying 'Told you so, cousin.' But I had put Jade's concerns to rest, along with mine, because I believed everyone deserves forgiveness. I never condoned what she did, but guilt and betrayal was hers to deal with. Karma too.

"I do. Olivia and I were going to grab some lunch and explore the city. I made dinner reservations for two later that I can adjust, if you care to join us."

"Um yeah, why wouldn't I?" she stated. "It's your birthday. Let me freshen up and I'll be right back down."

I nodded and smiled then turned to go grab my phone. I needed to change my dinner reservations before we started having too much fun and I forgot all about 'her lateness'.

"Quick question," she said, stopping me in my tracks. Her forehead was wrinkled as if she just remembered something. She twirled her finger clockwise. "What are all these camera people doing here?"

I had totally forgotten all about Olivia's folks being here, with Camille now showing up totally unexpected. She stared at me inquisitively while she waited for my response. My hesitation stemmed from me trying to put together the right words. Telling someone they might appear on a reality show that they didn't sign up for wasn't easy to blurt out.

"They're a film crew and they are here for Olivia, not us," I explained plainly.

"I'm sorry, say that again." Her eyebrows were not coming back down anytime soon.

"Camille, they're here for Olivia. She has a new reality show that she's on and they're here for her. I've already given them instructions that nothing personal should be recorded."

She let out a smug laugh.

"You can't be this naive, Ava...seriously? Have you seen a reality tv show? Do you really think they're going to adhere to that?" she asked snidely.

"They will if they don't want their entire network hit with a cease and desist. Followed by a lawsuit. Resulting in a big old settlement, okay?!"

Camille stared at me intensely.

"What's your angle?"

"Excuse me?" I was confused as to what she was getting at. "What do you mean, what's my angle?"

She eased closer to me. "Just like I said, what's your angle? Is this some kind of set up?"

For what? I wondered.

My forehead furrowed at her insinuating I was setting her up. We hadn't talked in, what, ten years, and yet here she was accusing me of setting her up. Who's got time for that?

"Camille, why the hell would I be setting you up? And with who?"

"You know what and who, don't play dumb, Ava."

Her tone was harsh and extremely accusatory. Whatever she was under the impression I was doing, I wasn't.

"Whatever little game you're playing, I want no parts of it. Keep that camera away from me, one hundred percent," was the last thing she said before she took off upstairs. Clearly she'd found a bedroom and made herself at home. I stood frozen at what just occurred. Then suddenly a tinge of the same annoyance I felt when Olivia showed up coursed through me.

'What the hell was that all about?' I thought, as I walked back into the living room to grab my phone. I had no idea what she was getting at. My telling her they were here for Olivia had obviously gone over her head. I pulled my phone out of my purse and scrolled to find the number for the restaurant.

Tonight was certainly going to be interesting.

As I lounged on a beach chair, soaking in the rays and the vacation vibes, my phone buzzed with a name I hadn't expected – Cameron. I sighed and took the call, bracing myself for the incoming melodrama.

"Happy birthday, Ava!" Cameron's husky voice came in strong across these miles, a little too cheery for my liking. He sounded so close that I literally looked over my shoulder, wondering if Olivia's film crew had set up some sort of surprise drop-in visit to amp up a twist for the episode.

"Thanks, Cameron. What's the real reason for this call?" I shot back, my tone as breezy as the ocean air swirling around me.

"No real reason, just wanted to wish you the best on your special day," he said, a hesitancy in his voice that betrayed an ulterior motive.

I took a sip of my drink, rolling my eyes. "Spit it out, Cameron. I'm on vacation, and drama is not on my itinerary."

He took a deep breath, and the words spilled out like a confession. "I miss us, Ava. I really miss you so much, baby. Maybe we can give it another shot."

My laughter bubbled up, echoing against the waves. "Cameron, you're a piece of work. I'm in Cabo, sipping cocktails and living my best life. I'm not interested in rehashing the past. My birthday wish? Leave me in peace."

The line fell silent for a moment before he stammered, "I thought maybe—"

Feeling like he had not heard me, I had no choice but to interrupt: "Save it, Cameron. You had your chance, and now you're just an outdated song on my playlist."

"Ava, hold on. I love you." He sounded sincere and sincerely sorry at the same time.

"I know you do, Cameron. I know you still love me, but the question is: does your fiancée?"

I let that hang for a bit and then gave him a hearty kiss off. "Adiós!" I ended the call, returning my focus to the turquoise sea and golden sands.

As the waves played their soothing melody, I couldn't help but reflect on the call. Cameron's attempt at a rekindling felt more like a desperate plea. In a way, it angered me that he had the nerve to try it. But to be perfectly real with myself, I was amused and slightly relieved to know I've still got it at forty. Despite everything that happened, he can't shake me off. So I *was* the love of his life. And his poor fiancée has no idea.

I chuckled, realizing how far I'd come since our messy breakup. The distant sound of the ocean drowned out the echoes of our history, leaving me with a sense of liberation. Some people just couldn't let go of the past, but for me, it was time to embrace the present and relish the birthday bliss that stretched out before me.

13

Chapter Thirteen: Happy Birthday, Ava

Olivia, Camille and I walked inside the restaurant, arms linked like we used to in the old days, making our grand entrance. Heads were turning left and right, and I could feel heat coming off of eyeballs all over the beautifully designed and elegant dining room. I'm sure there were some other ladies that were not as pleased to see us looking regal (and barely dressed) in our revealing sundresses and sandals. I noticed which husbands were the smart ones, the ones which picked up their menus and re-ordered drinks were likely happily married. The ones with their heads on a swivel were likely going to have some trouble in paradise.

I was instantly transported back to my first evening here. I was back at The Alexander for dinner again. The food was so spectacular the first time I came, I had to come back. The hostess, with a slight bit of attitude, peered down at the tablet to locate my name. Her fingers scrolled the list up until she found my name and stopped.

"Reservations for Richards," I said to the hostess.

"For three, si?" she asked, glancing back at me. She seemed to be taking in our outfits and I wasn't sure how to read her expression. Well, it was flat, giving nothing.

"Yes, that is correct."

"Okay, give me a few seconds," the hostess replied. "I want to make sure your table is cleaned and ready for you girls."

Its funny how 'girls' can mean different things, coming from different people at different times. Now having tipped the cusp of middle age, I might start requiring a little more respect to be put on my name. *Who you calling girl?* I remember how my mother and grandmother had to correct folks at times back in the day, in certain parts of town, where calling a grown woman a 'girl' was meant to be derogatory and a power move. I wasn't instantly offended by it, but it was a word on my watch list when it came to certain situations.

This didn't seem like such a situation. I had been treated so kindly by all of the staff at the resort so far, and with today being my birthday, I was hoping that the royal treatment would continue, if not be surpassed. So, Camille was not going to be the only diva tonight!

I nodded to the hostess, as she pressed down on her microphone that hung from her ear to verify. Peeking over my shoulder, I saw Camille pacing back-and-forth on the phone, while Olivia did what she needed to do for the show. She and Ian were off to the side of the entrance, with Olivia answering questions that Ian fired off rapidly to her, challenging her to make shady comments, and *'be funnier, louder Liv! Into the mic, please! C'mon Liv, give the people something to talk about!'* If I had to listen to Ian coach her all night, I just might scream.

Olivia seemed to enjoy it though, and she gave these mini monologues directly into the camera, about being on a girls' trip vacay and missing her kids, so much! But also being so, so happy to have some time away from the drudgery of domestic life: dishes, diapers, and vacuuming dog hair, daily.

I had no idea that Olivia was probably overwhelmed with her family lifestyle. In fact, maybe that was what made her seem distant and slightly disturbed? I guess this was my single black female privilege, I had no idea what it meant to have so many people depending on me daily for the little things in life. Being fed and clothed, being bathed and taught the basics of life. Parenting was no joke, obviously.

So I was glad to see Olivia taking some me-time, doing her show if that's what she wants, and living it up for a change. I was glad that I invited my old friends to come back and reconnect, despite the rocky start to this trip.

Admittedly, we'd had a pretty good day, notwithstanding Camille's little outburst earlier. I was still scratching my head about what that was all about, or why she felt I was colluding to trip her up or something.

My initial instinct was to address it before we left, but I decided to wait. Ruining my birthday by arguing with her was not something I cared to do. She had only been here less than twenty-four hours; I refused to let her take up all the space like she loved to do. Camille was the opposite of Olivia. Yes, they both were thirsty for attention, but for slightly different reasons. While Olivia suffered from mild to low self-esteem, Camille's was boiling over. If there were a human definition of braggadocious—it'd be Camille.

She loved being the center of attention, and she was truly hilarious in her own way, and most of the time would compete with us for the spotlight. The only person it consistently did rub the wrong way was Lauren. She used to always say how exasperating it was to live in Camille's world. Not that we did, but I understood where she was coming from.

If a guy looked at one of us, Camille had to make sure she did something to take his attention off of us and onto her. At times it was annoying, but it never really bothered me. It wasn't until she started doing her underhanded stuff, (violating girl codes—lying and sneaking—then including me, throwing me under the bus) well, that's when I had to draw the line.

Which is what had me ultimately questioning her real issue with the production crew following us around and recording every step. Was it jealousy or something else?

"Miss Richards," the waitress called out, interrupting my thoughts. "Please allow me to show you and your party to your table." Nice.

I signaled for them to follow, and the hostess glanced behind me. *Shit.* I knew who she was looking at before she uttered a word. I kept forgetting there were extra people traveling with us. An entire film crew, to be exact. Earlier I intended to remind Olivia to tell them to stay behind but forgot. Blame it on the margaritas– of course I had a few after that call with Cameron. My feelings had been all over the map in the last few hours.

I was excited to tell the girls about it – dish over the deliciousness that I was sure would be served up. Talk about having tea! I knew that there would be harsh opinions stated on an ex, who is *currently engaged*, reaching out *to rekindle things*. Honestly, Liv never liked him from day one, so I was all ears to have her bash him on my behalf.

The hostess abruptly stopped, turned and held up her hand, "I'm sorry, are they with you ladies?" Okay, that was better.

"They're with one of my guests," I answered.

"Are they filming something specifically?"

I was reluctant to respond. "Yes, it's for a reality show." Where was Ian? This was his matter to resolve. I warned him to get his ducks in a row, because I would not be responsible.

"I see," she paused, thinking of how she wanted to proceed, "I apologize for having to tell you this, but unfortunately we can't have any filming in the restaurant without prior authorization."

"I understand," I acknowledged, with a polite smile and a nod. Frankly, I felt relieved that someone else could step in and shut this down on my behalf. "Let me let her know."

I turned around to let Olivia know that her film crew wouldn't be able to come in.

"Hey, Olivia, unfortunately they're not letting the camera crew in. Something about not having prior clearance to do so."

"Seriously, Ava? They can't make an exception this one time? Can't you speak to the manager. Is he or she here?"

I sighed. This was the last thing I wanted to do on *my* birthday. Negotiate for her to have cameras when I really didn't care one way or the other. I wanted to roll my eyes so bad but I refrained. Olivia looked like a five-year old waiting to hear if she could have the extra scoop of ice cream or not.

I turned back around to speak to the hostess.

"Excuse me..." I glanced down at her name badge. "Valencia, would you mind speaking to your manager? My friend is filming a very popular reality show in the US, and I'm sure the restaurant being featured would be good for business." I know, I know. Tourists saying "in the US" are particularly annoying. Valencia would be in her rights to tell me, 'honey this ain't the US, we don't care nothing about no Evergreen Family Whatever' Or was that just me?

I put on my boss babe negotiator hat because that's what I do everyday at work, talk other bosses into discounting services, reselling those services at premium, and improving our bottom line. Not hard, not easy. I was successful in media because I was really good at talking things out, and therefore getting my way, that was a known fact in the industry.

But the raw truth was, here, on *my* vacay, I really didn't care. Personally, I preferred eating in peace—and getting 'its my birthday!' smashed— without a freakin' camera chasing every bite and sip down my throat.

She nodded. I could see the hesitation on her face.

"Give me a minute," she requested, stepping around the podium to locate her manager.

"Thank you."

"What did she say?" Olivia asked from behind me.

I faced her. "She's going to ask her manager, but don't hold your breath. I would suggest you keep them abreast of what's going on." I pointed to the crew.

Olivia turned to inform the crew of what was going on. Meanwhile, Camille continued her conversation as if nothing was happening. After a few minutes passed, the hostess returned with her manager.

"Good evening, I'm Donna, the manager. I was told you are a part of a reality show cast," she stated.

"No, I'm not." I turned to point at Olivia. "My friend in the blue dress is. Actually, she's the star."

Olivia saw me point at her and approached.

"I see," Donna said softly. "Well to be honest, we don't particularly delve in that arena due to the type of negative attention it garners; however, I spoke to the owner, and he's willing to make an exception, but only this one time. And there are conditions."

"Whatever they are, we will adhere to them," I promptly acknowledged.

Donna nodded. "Good. Your friend is allowed one camera and two crew members. That's all we can possibly make accommodations for, unfortunately. For capacity limits and liability reasons. We have to think of the comfort and safety of our other guests, even though we know this is a special occasion for you, I'm sure you understand?"

"Deal!" Olivia agreed excitedly. She rushed over to the crew to tell them the conditions.

Donna took note of Olivia's relief and then added the house rules. "There is also to be no yelling, screaming, expletives, or fighting whatsoever," she added. "I'm sure that goes without saying, among adults, but you would be surprised. Last month we had some Wives show taping here— just awful behavior all around!" Donna seemed to grit her teeth just recalling that experience. "But we trust you to enjoy the evening in a pleasant manner. Welcome."

I nodded vigorously in agreement. Normally, I'd be highly offended at a manager in an upscale restaurant attempting to berate us, bringing up the stereotypical behaviors she implied, but she wasn't lying. Nor was it race driven, as Donna was as brown and beautiful as the rest of our table. But unfortunately, she had every reason to be concerned about the typical behavior of reality show cast members, so stating what was not allowed was well within her rights as a manager.

"Thank you," I shook hands with the manager, just to confirm that she could trust us to be pleasant and not rowdy tourists who take advantage.

"You're most welcome." She smiled. "Valencia, please get them seated right away in our best ocean view table." Donna must have calculated that if she had to have us, the free publicity would be worthwhile if she gave us good treatment and excellent views. Why not generate some social media buzz for the restaurant?

When I took a second to officially follow Olivia on the gram— at her request, by the way— she had well over two million followers. I'm guessing someone at the resort must have noticed this by now as well. Luxury resorts, specifically their front desk agents, are notorious for googling their guests and finding out all of their preferences, and sometimes their secrets. Who do you think is always tipping off TMZ?

Valencia motioned for us to follow her. "This way."

As we weaved through the tables, I glanced around to observe what other people were eating, what looked delicious, so I could have an idea of what I might like to order. I saw very generously sized grilled lobster tails, beautifully layered ceviche in martini glasses, spreads of caviar on blini, overflowing charcuterie boards, and bottles of bubbly lodged in tubs next to most of the tables. The mood seemed to be refined and relaxed, which was promising.

"Dang that looks good," Olivia mumbled.

Everything looked so appetizing, I had to agree with her. At this point I didn't know what I wanted to eat. I had a taste for seafood, but when do I not? Nothing beats a fresh catch from the Pacific ocean, but the pappardelle bolognese was tugging at me too. Pasta is always so satisfying and could easily make the perfect birthday meal.

The hostess stopped indicating we'd arrived at our table.

"Here you are," she advised us, stepping back.

"Thank you," I replied, smiling. The water view of the sunset, the sounds of the buzzing Cabo marina and the yacht parties going on all around us generated an air of excitement. Perhaps this night was getting started in the right way after all, to celebrate my four decades of life well lived.

"Your server will be with you shortly." She waited for us to be seated then she walked back to the front.

"This is snazzy, girlfriend! Love this for me!" Olivia exclaimed, sitting down. "Have you been here before?"

I answered, "I came on my first night at the villa, and yes, I really liked it."

"Well the food must have been good if we're back," Camille added.

I air kissed. "Delicious! Divine!"

"Well let me check out this menu then because I am starving," Olivia announced.

We all scanned through the menu to figure out what we were selecting for the table.

"Good evening, ladies. What can I get you to drink?" he asked.

"I'll take an Old Fashioned, preferably with Hennessy XO if you have it—neat please," Olivia rattled off. "And a shot on the side." Oh, okay, this was a rather intense first drink order. As if we had not been sipping chardonnay all day at the beach, but sure.

Camille flashed Olivia a peculiar look. I almost did the same, but I kept my focus on the menu. Her drink order was rather strong starting off. I know it was my birthday and all, though if she drank like that all night, she'd be stumbling out of this restaurant. Part of me wanted to question her choice. She'd never been one to drink heavily. And with her film crew present, I would think she wouldn't want to be drunk off her ass on camera.

"I'll have a cantaloupe martini," I ordered. This was for old times sake, just to reminisce a bit. There was a season when this was the *hot-girl* cocktail choice, and I wanted to feel as much the *hot-girl* as I could tonight.

"That sounds great, I'll have the same," Camille agreed. She must also be remembering our club nights out in the city. "You okay over there, Liv?"

Olivia sipped her water. "Yeah, why?"

Her eyes roamed back-and-forth between me and Camille, waiting for someone to say something. I already knew there was something up with her. Normally I would've said something, but I was on vacation, it was my birthday, and what she drank was none of my business.

"Starting the party kind of early, that's all." Camille returned her attention back to the menu.

"We are celebrating a birthday, right?" Olivia asked. "Ava only turns forty once."

"Point taken," Camille agreed. "Soooo, ladies, what's been up? How's life treating you?"

"Life is good," I answered first. "I have a business merger on the verge of being finished, a new app launching, things are really good. Honestly, business is better than ever."

Camille sipped her water. Olivia smiled hearing my success. Speaking my successes out loud felt good. It felt rewarding. Most of the time I was honestly so busy, I hardly had time to even reflect on things. It was good to take stock of what I'd accomplished.

"Ava, that's amazing. I always knew you'd be successful." Olivia smiled at me. "You were always so focused and ambitious." I really loved, and appreciated, how she could give a genuine compliment with sisterly love, no trace of hating with Olivia. At least not towards me.

"Thanks, Liv, I'm proud of you too." I tapped her hand. "I can't wait to see your new show air! This is pretty damn cool!" I realized I should give her flowers as well, because not everybody is out here getting famous, so for better or for worse, she was making a name for herself. And over two million people knew her by name and followed her passionately. That's not nothing. I had to get out of my own snobbish head and acknowledge that she was living her own dreams, which is actually all that matters, right? She may not win an Emmy for this type of show, but the branding opportunities were endless. I mean, I of all people, should know from the marketing perspective, that she stands to make a great amount if she manages to stick with this thing.

"Speaking of which, what type of show is it by the way?" Camille asked snidely.

Olivia perked up. The excitement flooded her face as her eyes gleamed.

"It's a show about me and my life called Evergreen Family Values. Desmond and the kids will be on the show too," she said proudly.

"So it's not an actual television show, is this like a streaming thing?" Camille curtly added.

Her tone was condemnatory and quite frankly, shady as hell. I watched as Olivia deflated a bit. All it ever took was a slight diss and she would disappear. I knew it and so did Camille. Which is why she always pressed that button.

"Yes, it's on television!" Olivia snapped.

"Is it a network show, or?" Camille couldn't help herself. "Ava, do you get this? Am I crazy or what, because I never heard of this show."

Of course Camille assumed that if she hadn't heard of it, it was worthless. Camille prided herself on being 'in the know.' She honestly believed that as an event planner to a handful of famous people, she was now über connected and had the scoop on everything that happened, in NY, LA, DC and Miami. And if it didn't happen there, it didn't matter anyway. What a diva.

I smirked at the same time I saw the server returning with our drinks. The condensation dripped down the glass of my martini. He placed the glass down in front of me, the same for everyone else. Olivia's shot didn't touch the table for long at all before she had it raised to her lips, gulping down the amber-colored liquor as if she was trying to numb something. What, no toast? No cheers?

Slowly sipping my drink, I watched—as lovingly and non-judgmentally as I possibly could— as she picked up the other drink and started sipping heavily. Camille gave her a disapproving glare and I chuckled beneath my breath. I found it hilarious considering that when we would go clubbing on U Street, Camille herself used to throw shots back like an NBA player at the free throw line.

"Well, since we're talking about what we've been up to these days, let me fill you in on what I've been up to lately." She took a sip of her drink to hydrate herself before starting her long spiel. "I started an event planning business about eight years ago. Considering I was somewhat of a party girl, I figured I was an expert at parties."

Somewhat? More like the ultimate party girl.

I began, "That's good to he—"

Camille held up her finger to cut me off. "I wasn't finished. Like I was saying, I started an event planning business and it's been doing phenomenal. I've planned lavish parties for more celebrities than you can imagine, traveled around the world, and have fully secured the bag, as the kids say, strictly doing something I love." Wow. Way to lay it on! I was feeling second hand embarrassment for her lack of grace, and then I realized that this was mainly for the cameras. For Olivia's viewers. Camille sat here shamelessly plugging her event business on my birthday. Ugh!

Olivia signaled the server for another drink. She seemed entirely uninterested in what Camille was saying. I took another sip as Camille continued to brag about her life. My thoughts drifted off, as did my eyes across the restaurant. I glanced at all the decor. The other night I noticed how beautiful the decor was, wondering who came up with the concept and design. My eyes roamed towards the other side of the restaurant when I saw a familiar face.

I stared at him as he stood talking to someone at a table. The white jacket he had on hinted that he worked in the restaurant, in the kitchen. My eyes fixated on him as he conversed with the guests. When he turned slightly in my direction, I melted in my chair at the sight of all thirty-two of his perfect teeth. His megawatt smile was intoxicating. What's funny was I hadn't even noticed the dimple in his left cheek before. *How'd I miss that?* I felt like we had studied each other *pretty well* the other night. I sipped some more of my tasty martini, completely checked out of the conversation happening in front of me.

He must have had that feeling people always get when someone is staring at them, because he looked around until his eyes finally met mine.

I radiated my biggest and brightest, most inviting smile in his direction, and quietly murmured his name, "Tate."

14

Chapter Fourteen: Wine Goes Better with Infidelity

Our eyes locked as we stared at each other. I watched as the distance between us started to decrease as he moved closer to my table. The butterflies I felt the last time we were together began fluttering in my stomach once again. My smile grew even bigger as the view of him became clearer. I raked my eyes up-and-down his tall frame, stopping at his white chef jacket. On his right breast was the letter A in cursive writing with *Alexander* inscribed beneath it.

My eyes traveled to his left breast where *Chef Tate Ellington* was imprinted in the same script as the initial on the other side. Tiny breaths escaped through my partially agape lips as I stared in amazement.

Wait...he's the head chef. I said to myself, remembering now having seen his name at the bottom of the menu. I inhaled a long gasp of air when he finally stopped in front of me. I straightened up to appear as if I was keeping it together. I wasn't. Internally my inner schoolgirl was doing cartwheels. I resisted the urge to nibble on my bottom lip.

"Well hello, Ava," he said in a sultry tone that resonated all over my body. "You look absolutely gorgeous tonight."

Olivia's eyes widened impressively at the sight of him. Camille's neck turned in slow motion as her eyes drank him in. I fought the ascension of my cheeks, but it was no use. Tate's presence had a way of seizing control of my body temperature, causing my hormones to go haywire. I was doing all I could to regulate the pulsating I felt coursing over my skin.

"Hello, Tate," I said coyly. "And thank you."

I wanted to hug him, but I was afraid my knees would betray me if he touched any part of me or I got a whiff of his intoxicating masculine scent. Our previous encounter on the dance floor had my insides doing back flips from just a graze of his fingertips on my flesh.

His eyes glanced over my exposed skin before locking back on mine. The backless red dress I wore had already turned a few heads on our way to the table. But the way he looked at me...goodness gracious. I felt like the sexiest woman in the world right now.

I inhaled deeply, gradually exhaling the bated breaths. *Say something, Ava.* I searched my mind for something. Anything. The awkward silence filled with intense staring was thick. I blinked, breaking the spell to look at my friends who seemed to be interested in who this mysterious man was. The sly grin on Olivia's face confirmed that she'd put it together already. Camille's lustful gaze on the other hand was sizing up every angle of him.

"Happy Birthday Ava! once again!" Tate's comment definitely stirred up curiosity in both Olivia and Camille, who leaned towards each other. I could almost hear them saying, "Whaaat?" in their heads.

"How's your birthday going?" He finally cut through the awkward silence. "Did you enjoy your day?"

I nodded. "I did. It got off to an amazing start, and the entire day was really nice. I appreciate you asking." I had to drop that in so he that he knew I loved every second of last night.

"Of course." He smiled. "And I'm truly sorry about earlier, but we had a little kitchen emergency and I had to come into the office early," he waved his hand around the glamorous dining room as if to explain the magnitude of his responsibilities here.

"It's okay," I pointed to his left breast pocket. "By the looks of it, that emergency really was an emergency, you're the head chef?"

He placed his hand over his left breast. "Yeah, that's what happens when you're the boss. People call off and you have to jump in. The crises never seem to end."

I giggled.

"Being a boss is a gift and a curse," I added.

He winked. "Tell me about it."

We laughed together. I understood more than he knew. Suddenly, I became parched. I picked up my glass of water to quench my thirst. He had me inflamed beneath what I hoped and prayed was still a cool exterior. Backless dress or not, I may have started to perspire, because a lady never sweats, but I was feeling the heat between us.

Placing my water glass down, I returned my focus to him to see that he was still staring at me. I found it crazy how we were in the center of the room, in front of so many people, but just gazing at one another like no one else was even present.

"Ahem, ahem," Camille cleared her throat. "Ava, quit being rude and introduce us to your handsome chef friend." She held out her hand for him to shake. My focus shifted to her and the flirtatious expression plastered across her face. I glanced over at Olivia, as if to say, *'do you see this?'* then back at her.

"Camille, this is Tate. Tate, this is Camille and Olivia— the friends I was telling you about."

He shook Camille's hand and smiled at Olivia.

"It's nice to meet you both, ladies."

Camille held onto his hand a little longer than necessary and I fought the urge to smack it away. Which was crazy since he wasn't mine. Realizing she hadn't let go, he released her hand.

"So..." He clapped his hands together. "What are you having today? Have you decided on what dishes you might like to explore yet?"

I shook my head.

"No, I'm torn between the seafood options and the pasta, both are my favorites."

He grinned at me. I shuddered at the smoldering intensity of that smile.

"How about neither," he suggested.

I was highly intrigued. Let's play. Please, by all means, cook for me, Tate.

"Okay, then what would you suggest?"

He held out his hand signaling for me to hand over my menu.

"Something special for someone special on their special day," he answered. "I'm going to prepare you something amazing, just for you, that's not on the menu."

"You can do that?" Olivia asked.

"I can do whatever I want," he replied, boldly. "The Alexander is my place, its named for my father, who taught me everything I know, and I'm really glad you all are here." Tate gave me a wink and a nod, and I knew instinctively that he was already a step ahead of me. He might have planned this special menu instead of us meeting up for breakfast, and you know what, I was okay with that. Some special attention was right up my alley on the day of the grand rollover. Thirty nine to forty was worth an extra special dinner, calories be damned.

Camille's eyebrow arched at the same time as mine. I didn't have to be inside her head to know the wheels were turning. She had that look on her face. The look that meant her inner lioness was ready to pounce. And he was the prey.

"You certainly know how to charm a woman," I said, bringing the focus back to me. I held out my hand for their menus then handed them to Tate. "Whatever you prepare, we'll be happy to eat it."

The glimmer in his eye brightened.

"Do any of you have any allergies?" he inquired.

"Nope, not a single one," Olivia blurted out before sipping more of her drink.

"No," I said politely.

"I'll eat whatever you serve. And I mean whatever." Camille winked at him while smiling seductively.

Damn she has not an ounce of shame.

I shifted forward, and amped up my smile towards Tate. "Can I cash that rain check in later on?"

"Anything for the birthday girl." Tate reassured me that he was focused on me, despite Camille's petty, amateur and embarrassingly bold flirtations.

A sullen look flushed over Camille's face when she saw he perked up at my inquiry. *Bullseye.* I smiled inwardly at her look of defeat.

"Then it's a date," I told him.

He winked at me again. "What are you all drinking?"

"We're drinking Martinis," I waved my finger between Camille and my glass. "And she's drinking an Old Fashioned."

"Hennessy XO," Olivia added.

He laughed at her correction.

"I'll send over fresh drinks and a few appetizers while you're waiting on your entreés."

"Thank you, Tate."

He placed a gentle kiss on my cheek. "No problem."

* * *

"Dear God, that was the best thing I've ever eaten in my life," Olivia announced, tossing her napkin on the table before leaning back in her chair.

Tate had outdone himself preparing this Michelin-star quality meal for us. Since I couldn't decide between the pasta or the seafood, he fixed everything. Caribbean lobster tails with cheesy potato gratin and lemon remoulade sauce was just one of the mouth-watering entreés he indulged us with. Accompanying the succulent lobster we enjoyed a wood fired rib eye steak; seafood paella; a fisherman's platter of smoked snapper, prawns, sea bass, and roasted peppers; roasted sweet potato, truffle Yukon potato purée; salsa criolla and chimichurri sauce. Indulgent barely describes the plates and the presentation which were beyond belief and like nothing I've even had in Beverly Hills or Manhattan.

Olivia scraped her plate twice over, and tossed back four drinks. Camille and I were right behind her. Not only was Tate the head chef, he owned the restaurant too. I could only imagine what his lifestyle was like as both chef and owner, he had to be busy, and would he even have time to date? I was quite intrigued. The other night when we were talking, he never mentioned he owned a restaurant. He alluded to being an entrepreneur, but our conversation bounced around so much, I might've missed it.

I did have quite a bit to drink that night. I was also under the influence of more than just alcohol as well. All of my worry about turning forty and here I was. The day had come, and so far, so great.

"Good Lord, Ava. Looks like you snagged quite the catch," she complimented me. "He's tall, dark, handsome, and he can cook. Chiilllleee, he definitely checks off several boxes in my head. Throw in the fact that he owns his own business too...yes, girl, get your black king."

She snapped her fingers back and forth approvingly. I belted out a laugh. Olivia was tipsy as hell, but that didn't take away from her being funny. "Thanks, girl, but we're just acquaintances. I just met the man." I was being coy but inside I was dancing to the beat of Naughty Girls, by Beyonce. I knew what I had hoped would be my birthday gift by now.

"Tonight, I'll be your naughty girl..."

I imagined Tate picking up on my subtle waves of seductive energy, and then I wondered if it was just this martini taking over my good sense.

Camille peered over the rim of her glass. She was taking it all in. Assessing the situation. I could see the invisible wheels turning in her head without actually being inside of her head. When you know a person for years, it works that way. Her silence spoke volumes. Her eyes too.

"So he's single?" Camille questioned.

"As far as I know, but I'm not here for all that," I told her. "I came to relax and reconnect with my friends." I smiled warmly at both of them, actually feeling an even deeper gratitude for their presence tonight.

"I see. Then you don't mind if I slide him my digits? On a professional tip, of course."

Olivia snickered.

"Damn, girl, you are still bold as hell." She finished off her cocktail and looked across the table at Camille. "Are you really going to act like you didn't see that man undressing Ava with his eyes?"

"Are you going to act like you didn't just hear Ava say that they're acquaintances? And she just met him. It's not like they're dating. And last I checked, single means available." Camille gave Olivia a sassy look.

"Apparently so does being married," Olivia mumbled beneath her breath.

Camille's brow furrowed. "Excuse me?"

We both stared at Olivia, waiting for her to respond. She looked around and I knew she was looking for the waiter so she could order another drink.

"Desmond is cheating on me," she revealed, then finished the rest of her drink. "At least that's what my gut is telling me."

I immediately looked at the two guys on her crew.

"Can you all give us a moment please?" I asked them. I had a feeling she wouldn't want this on film. "I'll come get you in a few."

They bobbed their heads, lowered the camera, and stood to leave.

"Thanks," I said.

I turned my attention back to Olivia once they exited. Staring at her, my words were stuck in my throat. I searched for the right words to say, to be comforting, compassionate, but I couldn't conjure up anything. I wanted to be shocked; however, I wasn't. This wasn't new news. But I didn't have the heart to tell her that. Silence floated between us. There had been plenty of things I'd dealt with in my relationship with Cameron, but infidelity wasn't one of them.

Besides, what do you really say in a situation like this?

"Olivia, I–I–I," I stuttered searching for the right words, "I don't know what to say."

Tears welled up at the bottom of her eyelids. All night she had been drinking to mask her feelings and it seemed they had still fought their way past the armor of liquor. I caressed her arm as she shielded her eyes with her hand. Her expressions reflected the usual emotions; hurt, betrayal, and naturally, embarrassment—which I understood. Guess I was surprised she openly admitted it. Just this morning, she was denying anything was wrong, now this.

Olivia wiped the tear that fell on her cheek away. My eyes shifted to the steady rate her chest rose and fell as she tried to breathe through the deep pain that she was doing her very best to contain. I peeked over at Camille. She had a face of stone. Not an emotion in sight. Her eyes found mine before looking back at Olivia.

This felt like twelve years ago all over again. Except this time she knew or at least she was paying attention.

"When did you find out?" I asked.

She looked at me. "That's the thing, I haven't found any concrete evidence yet."

"Are you sure then?" I asked, believing that, unfortunately, her suspicions were more than likely all too valid. Desmond had always been a problem in my opinion.

"I've suspected for a long time, I guess I just ignored it. Maybe it was the money. Or the fact that he spoiled me. Or possibly, because when we weren't at odds, he made me feel special. I don't know."

More tears fell from her eyes.

I know the feeling, I silently agreed, thinking back to my relationship with Cameron. Some men had a way of seducing and manipulating your feelings until you questioned your own rationality and common sense. *'Been there, sister'* is what I wanted to say to Olivia, but I felt that would be making the moment too much about me. I've been accused of this too in the past.

"I need to be excused," she said, standing up. "I'll be right back."

I nodded as she walked off to gather herself.

The moment she was out of sight, I peered over at Camille who hadn't offered a word of encouragement or sympathy. Sitting back, I crossed my leg and rotated my body in her direction. She stared back at me. For some reason, I couldn't quiet the thoughts that were racing through my mind.

"You're awfully quiet," I pointed out.

"What would you like me to say, Ava?" Camille locked eyes with me, frowning.

I pursed my lips.

"Camille, I'm going to ask you this one time, and one time only. Are you sleeping with Desmond?"

She glared at me. Eyes full of contempt as a scowl formed across her lips.

"Are you really sitting here asking me this?"

"It's a simple question. Are you sleeping with Desmond? And let's not act like what I'm saying is so out of the realm of possibility or offensive."

She leaned onto the table. The previous scowl on her face shifted into a condescending smirk. "First off, I don't have to answer any of your questions. Secondly, no I'm not sleeping with him. And lastly, I don't appreciate the accusation."

I examined her. Searching her eyes for the lie I felt she was telling. She'd always been a good liar. Camille could talk her way out of anything. It was a wonder she went into event planning instead of pursuing politics. I rested my chin on my hand. There was something about this that didn't add up.

"Why are you staring at me like that?" she asked brashly.

"I don't know. Guess I'm wondering if you're telling the truth or not. You were pretty upset earlier about the film crew being here, and I couldn't for the life of me figure out why. Now that she's claiming Desmond is obviously cheating on her, I wonder if that's why you felt I was setting you up. Seems pretty coincidental to me, don't you think? Especially since I'm fairly certain you never told her *the truth*."

She scoffed at my observation.

"You know, Ava, I should've known you hadn't changed. I don't know why I bothered coming. You're still the same controlling, judgmental person you were all those years ago. It's no surprise why Lauren didn't come."

Classic Camille.

I swallowed. Her comment cut deep. I turned my head, eyes closed, as I tried to push the hurt down. Camille had a way of driving the invisible knife in and twisting until you couldn't take it anymore. But I knew better. And I knew this was nothing more than her deflecting.

I turned back around to face her when I peeped Olivia headed back our way.

"You can deflect all you want, Camille, but we both know the old saying, *what happens in the dark, comes to the light.*" I smiled smugly at her. "Betrayal has a price. Karma don't play. I hope you're telling the truth."

15

Chapter Fifteen: Morning After Guilt

C amille's denials and our exchange of words stuck to my heart like a band-aid all through the night. I tried to shake them off, but I couldn't. They wouldn't let me go. They tugged at my heart strings. Pulled roughly at my conscience. The same went for the guilt I felt regarding Olivia's situation. For the first time since landing in Cabo, I was having extreme trouble sleeping again, tossing and turning. I could sleep for an hour, wake up and lay there in bed, sweating, heart racing, and theorizing about what was happening in all of our lives. Hours passed with no rest at all.

"I think my friend is sleeping with my other friend's husband," I confessed to him.

"Whoooaaa," Tate said, looking at me, eyes wide.

Shock riddled his expression.

We had planned to meet on the beach to watch the sunrise together. After dinner I was emotionally drained and suggested we could meet in the morning. He happily obliged since it'd been a very long day for him too. I was appreciative of the crazy amount of effort he had put into creating a the birthday dinner of my dreams. I could still taste the amazing flavors in my mind and the cravings were already building.

I sipped the coffee he brought with him as the sound of my words echoed in my head.

"Wow, your two friends that I met last night? What makes you think something like that?"

I leaned my head on his shoulder.

"Because she crossed a line a long time ago. And I thought she had stopped, but something inside of me is telling me she hasn't."

"Did you ask her?"

I nodded.

"She said she wasn't."

"And you don't believe her?"

I sat up to look at him. "I want to, but it's why we fell out all those years ago. I found out and told her she needed to stop and come clean. In true fashion, she threw a fit, pointed the finger at me, then told me to mind my business."

"Have you told the other friend?" he inquired. I got the sense that he was trying to withhold judgment but frankly, I could sense what he *really* thought about it.

"No." I frowned shamefully. "I felt truly torn between them. How do you tell one friend the other friend is sleeping with her man without feeling like you're betraying either of them?"

"That's a hell of a predicament to be in, Ava. And to have it dropped like a bomb on your birthday...ouch."

"Tell me about it."

Tate wrapped his arm around me, pulling me closer to him. His embrace comforted me. We sat in silence for a few minutes. Breathing in the fresh air. Thinking about a reasonable approach to this extremely complicated situation.

I lifted the hot coffee to my lips. The robust Mexican blend warmed me up from the inside, helping me to calm down and relax. Tate caressed my arm as I laid on his shoulder. I didn't know what to do. I had no proof that Camille was the other woman, the villain in Olivia's miserable situation, so I couldn't say anything. Then there was my culpability in all of this. I knew about Camille and Desmond's illicit affair years ago and said nothing. That's what made all of this so extremely hard for me now. Especially to have this rear its ugly head on my birthday, when I just wanted to have a fresh start with my girls, but no, the old drama strikes again.

"I don't know what to do, Tate," I admitted. "I know it was foolish to have them both come on the vacay, but to tell you the truth, I didn't know if either would show up. I didn't know what I was doing planning this, I just know I wanted to see my girls again. What can I do?"

"There's nothing *you* can do. She denied it and if you don't have proof it's her, bringing up old dirt from the past won't mean anything. I mean, sure she'll know now, but that doesn't solve her current problem." Tate seemed so level headed and calm about this, but that was easy because these aren't his friends, and we just met.

"I know." I sighed. "I supposed I thought she'd realize that betraying someone she's been friends with since childhood over a sleazy guy wasn't worth it."

He huffed softly.

"What?" I glanced up at him.

"You know, I had someone tell me a long time ago, the way you view people and your relationship with them, may not be even close to how they view it." It stung hearing it, but once I got past my feelings, I realized then that he was right. I held certain people in a different light than they obviously held me. And so did Camille, perhaps she never saw Olivia as her friend in the first place. That should have been obvious, but I'm just fully seeing it now.

I smiled faintly.

He sounded more like Jade than I cared to admit. Jade's outside viewpoint of my friendships looked very different than my internal one. Jade always felt there was some underlying jealousy there, but I denied it. We'd been friends too long, and we were all equally talented and intelligent, so I could never fully embrace that perspective.

"May I ask you something?" he asked me.

"Sure, of course you can."

"What was it about these friendships that made you feel like they were worth saving?" he probed. "I mean, it sounds like they're pretty toxic."

Ouch. I didn't know why his comment bothered me, but it did.

"We have history," I told him. "A lot of history and memories—good and bad."

He nodded slowly.

"That sounds like what people say when they're asked why they hold onto a relationship when their partner is mistreating them."

I smirked. "I see what you did there."

"It's the truth. We don't look at friendships the same way we look at romantic relationships, but in reality, they're no different. Actually, sometimes they're far more intense. Sometimes they last much longer, and the breakups are just as severe."

I took another big sip of coffee, as last night had been another situation where I was over served. "You're a thousand percent correct." I exhaled a long, labored breath and stared out into the horizon. I wished life was as perfect as this scenery right here. Gazing out into the horizon, admiring the shimmering turquoise water, I reflected on the magnificence of God's amazing creation.

I squeezed his arm. "If only life was as simple as nature."

"Life is pretty simple. We humans complicate it."

"Right again." I nudged, staring up at him. "Let me find out you're some kind of scholar or something."

He laughed at my teasing. Then looked down at me and I froze for a moment. Being this close to him, breathing in his air, it was calming. Soothing. Arousing. Yet his presence relaxed me in a way that I hadn't felt in a long time. We held our stare for a few seconds before he inched his face closer to my lips. When I didn't flutter, he continued.

His lips pressed against mine softly. Gently. With ease, he gracefully moved them back-and-forth against mine. Then slowly, he slid his tongue between my lips. We paused. Reveling in the moment before delving further. Our sensual entanglement started off unhurriedly, then his hand gripped the back of my head, and he took over. Greedily tasting me. Savoring the sweetness. Relishing the moment.

I was under his full control. My body involuntarily found itself lifting off the ground and straddling him. My knees planted in the sand as his hands held onto both sides of my head. Our kiss was fervent. Wild. Sexy. I moaned inside of his mouth, unable to exhale since my mouth was under siege by his lips.

His hands moved slowly downward, gripping my hips to press me in even closer into his lap. I was lost in the moment. Tate tasted like a rare sweetness, and I wanted as much of it as I could handle.

Minutes passed by before I finally broke the kiss, exhaling loudly to give my lungs the air they desperately needed. His eyes contained a ravenous gaze that sent electricity shooting through me. I had never had a man stare at me with such passion, such a yearning. I couldn't tell if he wanted to taste or simply devour me.

The only sound between us was our rapid breathing. Even the sound of crashing waves had completely faded away and beyond my attention. We wallowed in momentary peace while we tried to grasp the full meaning of what just occurred. The kiss was bound to happen. The chemistry between us was electrifying. Our occasional glances spoke louder than our words at times. It was only a matter of time before this happened.

And now that it had happened, what now?

"Tate," I purred.

My lips were still within inches of his. Close enough that his breath grazed the outer layers of mine. He held my butt cheeks in the palm of his hands, and they felt good there. Surprisingly they felt like they belonged there. I placed my hand on his chest. His heartbeat raced beneath my touch. Hurried. Quickened. Oddly in sync with mine.

"Yes," he uttered seductively.

"I actually need to go," I whispered, with regret. "My friends are waiting for me."

"Not yet." He seized my lips again. This time with even more passion than before. I exhaled slowly, and melted into the moment. I knew the girls were waiting back at the villa, but I didn't want to stop. I couldn't. The feeling, his touch, it all felt too good to be true.

I delved into this abyss of euphoria a little while longer before parting.

I giggled. "I really have to go, Tate. Although I don't want to leave you."

"Okay fine," he pouted. "If you just have to go."

I smiled as I nibbled on my bottom lip. He poked his lip out. His mini tantrum was adorable. I placed a peck on his lips before climbing off his lap. I stood up and held out my hand to help him up. He took it and I pretended to assist in pulling him up. Once his feet were planted, he pulled me back in for a hug, wrapping his arms around my waist.

He placed another kiss on my lips. "Come on, I'll walk you back to your villa."

I complied by taking his hand as we walked up the beach hand-in-hand, arms swinging, a coquettish smile plastered all over my face. Tate felt like everything was right in the world. And I needed some happiness. A little joy. A lot of love.

The walk to my place was a short one since we met just at the bottom of the hill from my villa. He embraced me one last time before kissing me tenderly.

"Catch you later?" he asked.

"Definitely," I replied, winking.

Our arms slid down the others in slow motion until our connection was broken. I walked into the house and watched until he disappeared. I touched my lips, already missing his.

"Girl, I can't believe it's been so long!" I overhead Camille shout.

I turned around, confused as to who she could possibly be talking to. After dinner last night, I knew there was no way she was happily chatting with Olivia. The farther I got into the house, the louder the chatter became. I rounded the corner into the kitchen to see the three of them around the large marble island. Olivia saw me and smiled. I noticed then that she was looking at something across the room and turned to see what she was staring at.

The bliss I felt not even five seconds ago had instantly shifted.

"Ava."

"Lauren."

What do you call that feeling when you think you're over a thing and then it comes flooding back to you at full speed when you least expect it? Oh, that's right. Resentment. Aha! So Lauren made it down to Cabo after all. The day *after* my birthday.

16

Chapter Sixteen: The Bull and The Ram

"Lauren."

"Ava," she repeated.

I twisted my lip to the side. One would think after three days of random pop ups, I would be used to people just showing up after they said they weren't coming, or agreed to come, then temporarily vanished—but I wasn't.

However, I was surprised.

Lauren had always been a very absolute person. When she said something or made a decision, nine times out of ten, she stood on it. Very true to her sign of Taurus. So to see her comfortably seated at the island, laughing like she didn't outright decline my invitation left me stumped. Confused, nonetheless.

I searched for something to say. Everyone's eyes were on me. Olivia looked as though she'd been caught off guard too. Camille appeared quite happy she was here. Meanwhile, Lauren and I were stuck in a Mexican standoff, fittingly. I had mixed emotions, same as when Camille arrived, that much I could admit. Five days into my vacation and suddenly she shows up. I couldn't decide whether I should dwell on the disrespect or let it go.

"You look surprised to see me," Lauren finally said.

I huffed beneath my breath. Taking her presence in. Lauren was still a pretty girl, but quite a bit more rounded out these days. Where she was once enviably slim in our college years, her body had clearly changed now that we were approaching middle age life. She now embodied the coke bottle image that lots of people were paying surgeons thousands for these days. Although Lauren's updated shape might have been compliments of her three kids, I suspected. Her razor-cut bob stopped just shy of her jawline, highlighting a very sculpted face, which I suspected had botox-assistance. Lauren had always been the natural beauty of our crew, so I was surprised to see her looking, well, so professionally groomed, I guess you could say.

"Lauren, can I speak to you in the other room for a moment?" I requested.

She hesitated slightly, as if contemplating if she even wanted to entertain what was about to occur.

Once we were in the other room, we stared at each other for a few moments. I honestly didn't know how to feel. We hadn't seen each other since before her wedding. So that was a lot of years, and I had never met any of her kiddos in real life, which was pretty sad. The sheer fact that she hopped on a plane and flew down here without so much as a peep baffled me.

If there was one thing I could say about my friends with absolute certainty, it would be that they knew how to make an entrance. Heck, they also knew how to exit stage left pretty well also.

"You decided to come after all," I stated, still eyeing her.

"I did," she answered, with a bit of an attitude.

"And you didn't feel the need to notify anyone? Mainly me." *Hello, the host!*

"My decision to come happened at the last minute," she replied in her typical 'I do what I want, so deal with it' tone. I gritted my teeth to restrain myself from flying off the handle. "You sent me the info with an open-ended invitation, might I add; therefore, I didn't think I had to report my decision to change my mind." She gave me a mischievous half-grin.

And there it is: that spiteful smirk. That look of pure pettiness.

I looked on as she stood with her hand on her hip.

Her calculated response ruffled my feathers.

Lauren was an actual, factual know-it-all. Stubborn. Strong-willed. Always had been. Which is why we often bumped heads growing up. Without fail she wanted to be the one who always made the decisions. The three of them would swear on the Bible that I was the control freak, but in reality, it was Lauren. Her need for perfection usually incited most of our disagreements.

"It's not a matter of you changing your mind, rather it's a simple matter of you being courteous," I shot back. My temperature was rising but not in the good way that Tate had caused just minutes ago. Is this what a hot flash would feel like? Because I was starting to feel rising resentment burn in my chest, and I couldn't hold back. "Especially since the trip was paid for. It's you being considerate honestly."

I was over all of them just *popping* up. Although she and Camille did initially decline, and Olivia agreed to come, none of them had thought enough to give me at least a heads up that they changed their minds, and quite frankly, I was pissed off about it. And I guess I hadn't realized how much until she showed up today. Which I also knew was purposefully done.

Because she could have easily come yesterday instead. On my actual birthday. The reason that she was invited in the first place. The passive aggressiveness was off the charts.

"My, my, my, if it isn't the pot calling the kettle black."

"Excuse me?" I narrowed my eyes. Her smug tone had me 'five minutes off her ass', as Jade liked to say. "I think I misheard you."

"You didn't and I said what I said," she reiterated.

Oh! What?

My neck coiled at her blatant rudeness. Bemusement swept over my face as I tried to make sense of her aggressiveness and her stank attitude.

"Is there something you want to get off your chest?" I asked bluntly. "Because if there is, please by all means, spit it out. I'm here to have a good time, it is *still* my birthday week, so I'm not with the BS today Lauren."

Lauren's brow furrowed at the sharp change in my disposition. It had been many years since she experienced the tougher side of me, but I didn't build up my business by taking crap, that's for sure. My intention was never to pull her in here to be confrontational, but it appeared that's what she came here for, so I was ready for whatever.

"I don't need your permission to speak my mind, Ava."

"I never said you did, Lauren." I made sure to put as much emphasis on her name as she did mine. "However, if you have something to say, don't bite your tongue on my behalf."

Her jaw tightened as she glared at me.

I continued. "Look, if you came here on some bullshit, you can leave. I have been enjoying my trip despite all of you showing up whenever you felt like it. Which. Is. Rude." I paused to gather myself, breathe and get grounded. I had to will myself to push back the fear of heart palpitations and having a panic attack, from the emotional toll of all of these events which were outside of my control. I resolved that I would ease up on the confrontations, even if there was a part of me that wanted everything out on the table. "So if there's nothing else, I'd like to get back to vacay mode."

"Typical Ava. You always want people to jump when you say jump, but you don't do the same for others. It doesn't feel good when people don't show up for you does it? When they miss key moments in life that you can never get back."

A baffled look overtook my facial expressions. I was getting really tired of the *typical Ava* comments. It was obvious Lauren had some pent-up issues she needed to get off her chest, and I was fine with that, but this wasn't the way. She'd been here a hot minute and we were already at each other's throats. I was back to wishing none of them had shown up at this point. My time with Tate had been bliss, and this— this reunion and 'sister bonding time'— had gone all the way left and I was so over it.

"Again, if there's something you want to say, say it. Otherwise, miss me with the passive-aggressive shade." I was going to be firm and decisive, despite promising to leave work Ava in Los Angeles, I was forced to defend myself.

She pursed her lips at me. Silence resonated between us. Her eyes squinted like they used to when the tiny wheels in her head started turning. Lauren knew her Queen B attitude was no match for mine. I could verbally spar with the best of them. The worst too. I waited as she decided what she wanted to do. Folding my arms across my chest, adjusting my posture, I stood across from her ready for whatever. Lauren was undoubtedly a stubborn Taurus, but I was true Aries. Fiery. Quick-tempered. Straightforward. Not at all shady like Lauren, who wouldn't just say what bothered her, and she also carried a grudge like nobody's business.

Our sun signs clashed more often than not.

I knew what she was pissed off about. I'd known for years, but if she wasn't bold enough to speak her mind, that was on her. But I wasn't going to be disrespected. And she sure as hell wasn't going to ruin my fortieth birthday trip.

I am a grown woman. This had become my new mantra, my mirror pump up chant. Nobody can tell me what to do, I am a grown woman. Ha!

I arched my eyebrow to indicate anytime she was ready to speak, I was ready to listen.

"The floor is yours," I told her.

She peered at me over the sunglasses perched on her nose, for a little while longer.

Sighing heavily, she finally said, "Don't even worry about it," then waved me off.

I relaxed my face a little. Still keeping my defenses up until I was sure she was done with the pettiness. Unfolding my arms, I exhaled the elongated breath I'd been holding onto. To think I had a great morning only to come back to this.

"You sure?" I confirmed. "Because now is the time, since I don't plan on spending the rest of this vacation dodging your shade."

"I said don't worry about it."

Her tone had shifted from the bitchiness it carried before, to the stern, maternal tone I assumed that she used with her kids. I nodded to confirm we were moving past it. *For now,* I thought knowing good and well that we'd be revisiting this conversation sooner rather than later. One tequila shot is probably all it will take.

"How about we call a truce for now," she suggested. And despite looking well put together, Lauren's eyes looked tired. I recognized that look all too well. "There's a lot we should catch up on, Ava. A lot." I heard the sadness just then, and I took it in. "I mean, girl, I just got off a rather long flight, to come see y'all, and I thought that was the point of this gathering, to let our bygones be bygones? Release the past, no?"

I shrugged lightly. "I'm good with that if you are."

"I am." She relaxed her stance. "What were you all getting into today?"

"There's a pool party at the resort club. I reserved a private cabana with all the amenities, champagne, open bar."

"Okay! That's what I'm talking about Ava!" Lauren perked up just a bit.

"Yes, ma'am. The plan is to get lit- and forget all this bullshit." I quipped and gave her a slightly thawed out grin. "Look, Lauren, thanks for coming down to Mexico, *although extremely late.* You're most welcome to join us— *hey, we are all trying and that's what really matters*, so let's enjoy this time."

She gave me a faint smile.

"Sounds like a plan to me."

17

Chapter Seventeen: Broken Treaties

The pool party was in full swing by the time we arrived at our cabana. We were delayed waiting for Olivia to finish with her glam squad and finally be camera ready. I swiveled my head left and right as I walked the pool deck. Everywhere we turned there were people dancing, laughing, and drinking fruity cocktails, which looked deliciously inviting. There was also quite an arrangement of eye candy. Men of all heights, shades, and muscular builds were spread out across the multi-leveled infinity pools. My eyes moved like windmills trying to take it all in. Woohoo, I needed this vacay.

I spotted the section I had reserved. *Nice.* I smiled at how large the area was. Tate invited me to the pool party and encouraged me to bring along my friends to help lighten the mood and, hopefully, distract Olivia from her drama. He even pointed out how it could possibly be good footage for her reality show. That comment alone made me slightly reluctant to attend. The last thing I wanted was to be enjoying myself, have too many drinks, let loose and later see my ratchet behavior posted all over the internet. I wished that I could unfriend TikTok and Instagram sometimes, like, what ever happened to privacy?

"Here we are," I waved at our section, scooting to the side for them to walk in and get settled on the chaise lounges.

"Now this is what I'm talking about, some fun!" Olivia shouted over the music. "Point me in the direction of the bar. I'm feeling like indulging in brown liquor and a few of these brown men, honey."

I laughed at her eagerness to turn up. To be honest, I was glad she was feeling better or at least pretending to be. Dropping a bomb such as the one she dropped last night was pretty heavy. I had no personal experiences with a cheating partner, but I was sure it wasn't a pleasant feeling to sit with.

Camille pulled her dark glasses down to peek over at Olivia. To me, it was an indicator that she was observing her state of mind, but why would she do that unless she had a stake in this matter? When Olivia revealed all, she hadn't had a care in the world, no concern whatsoever.

"How about you take it a little easy today," she insisted. "Especially with the dark liquor. You already took a gummy."

Olivia shooed her. "Camille Diana Walters, you're not my parent or guardian. And I'm grown, so find you some business that doesn't require you acting like my AA sponsor."

"Not her government name," Lauren said, fighting the urge to laugh.

"Right. She was serious with it," I added.

Camille rolled her eyes.

"Whatever. I was just trying to help you out. But you go right ahead and be a city girl on national television if you want. Better you than me."

"Thanks," Olivia gladly dismissed her. "Now where's the waiter?"

"I ordered bottles, Liv," I informed her.

She leaned to the side with some sass.

"Okay, girl, ball out then. I'm trying to be like you. Where the money resides, where the money resides." She rocked side-to-side, snapping her fingers.

I chuckled at her goofiness. Lauren shook her head grinning. Everyone knew Olivia was the group comedian. And when she had liquor in her system, the jokes were never ending. It was just a part of her free-spirited nature.

Olivia walked to the edge of the cabana's deck.

"Now, let's see what we're working with. There's a whole lot of melanin and muscles out here." She lifted her sunglasses up. "I'm predicting sunny weather with a hundred percent chance of chocolate thunder...oowww."

I busted out laughing. Lauren joined in. Camille kept her resting bitch face which made me side-eye her. I was trying to grasp why she was so bothered by Olivia's unbothered disposition. I would think she'd be happy she wasn't moping around, spoiling everyone else's fun.

"Did you forget you were married?" Camille asked.

Olivia rolled her neck around to face Camille. Resting her hand on her hip before she turned up her lip at Camille's nosiness.

"Damn, Camille. First you're policing my alcohol intake, now you're regulating who I can *look at, at a pool party, on vacay?* Chile, please." Olivia looked flushed with anger, and like she was about to hit the roof of the cabana. "Girl, go find you some business so you can stay out of mine."

She had that coming. I turned my head and snickered. Usually Lauren was the mother hen, but Camille seemed to be embracing that role today, but no one was buying it.

Camille pointed her finger at her. "Um, I'm only looking out for you, chick. You're the one with a show centered around *family values*," she sarcastically air quoted. "So maybe let's not act like we're at Freaknik. Especially since we're unwilling participants in this ruse now."

Olivia stepped to Camille.

"Alright, alright...everyone to their corners," Lauren motioned.

"Camille, what's up with you? And Olivia...did I miss something? What show?"

Olivia returned to where she was standing, ignoring Lauren's question, and dismissing Camille. "I'm going to the bar. I need a shot now before I slap her silly behind," Olivia announced, stepping down to head towards the bar I saw at the opposite end when I was looking for our section.

I glanced over at Camille then shook my head. Something had obviously ruffled her peacock feathers, and I wasn't about to inquire as to what, since I had an idea why she was being a bitch. The *ruse* reference was low, and she was being spiteful. And there was only one explanation for it.

She was jealous of Olivia.

For several reasons, but I'd bet my last dollar her marriage to Desmond was the main reason. "Camille, maybe you should take a walk. Apparently, you have some tension built up." I suggested as I sat down. "Perhaps a dip in the pool or ocean to cool off."

"No one asked for you to shift into fixer mode, Ava Pope."

Camille rolled her eyes and left. Lauren glanced over her shoulder, stifling her laugh to see my hands up.

"What's her problem?" she asked, sitting next to me. "Or shall I say, their problem?"

"Your guess is as good as mine."

I shrugged off her comment because I didn't want to get into it. I had an idea what the problem was, but as Olivia pointed out earlier, it was none of our business. And since I didn't have actual evidence to prove that she was the mysterious mistress, or that Olivia even wanted her business blasted, or Camille's real hang up; I was staying out of it.

"Have they been like this the whole time?" she continued to probe.

"No! In fact, today is the first day. They were fine before you arrived." I clenched my teeth the moment the comment left my lips.

148

"What's that supposed to mean?" We were inching back to the conflict in the villa.

"Nothing. I didn't mean it like that, Lauren." I attempted to clean it up. "What I meant was they were fine last night, and I came back to all of you in the kitchen talking, so I'm not sure where the problem stemmed from. They were fine before."

She stared at me for a few seconds before nodding. I breathed softly, relieved that she took the high road. I really hadn't meant for it to come out that way. Lauren stood up abruptly and straightened her linen cover up.

"I'm going to walk around for a second. I'll be back."

"Okay," I said as she disappeared like the others.

* * *

"Cabo, are you with me?!" the DJ shouted into the microphone. "Let me hear you!"

I raised my hand and yelled along with the crowd. Screams echoed throughout the crowd as everyone danced and partied. We had been here a few hours now, laying in the sun, floating on giant swans in the massive pool, and the party was still going strong. After the awkward start when we first arrived, all of the girls eventually mellowed out. Thanks to a few rounds and, for Olivia and Lauren, some tropical flavored hookah.

At last, I had a chance to see Tate one-on-one.

"Your body feels good against mine," Tate whispered erotically in my ear.

You feel good too.

"Same," I managed to say.

He squeezed me tighter. I blushed while taking another sip of my passion fruit and hibiscus margarita. I'd lost count at this point. The way his warm breath felt on my skin with this tequila coursing through my system was next level. My back was pressed against his torso as he held me close to him. Normally, I wouldn't have allowed this much touching from someone I wasn't in a relationship with, but he was different.

He was *Tate.*

And Tate had a way of making me toss my inhibitions to the wind, right along with caution and step outside of myself. He showed up a couple hours after we did and found me in the crowd. Since then, we'd been all up under each other. We took turns walking back-and-forth between his cabana and mine. As luck would have it, his was directly across from mine, so I was able to still keep an eye out for my friends.

The business woman in me was always concerned about liability and lawsuits, and since my girls were here at my invitation, I needed to keep watch over it all. Or was I actually being, what they called, controlling Ava? Did I need to loosen up a bit? Well, too many women on vacation have gone missing in Mexico for me to stop being controlling or whatever you want to call it. Someone has to watch our backs.

Proving my point, Olivia had turned all the way up before the sun was even due to set. Between the mixed drinks, hookah, and gummy she ingested earlier, she was already on Jupiter. Her vibe regardless of her circumstances was pure Black girl joy. Lauren was dancing and laughing as well. But not nearly as much as Olivia. That wasn't a surprise though. Lauren was never one to get as tipsy as the rest of us. Her limitations on being wild were due to her needing to maintain her 'everything is perfect' façade. And yet, we all remember freshman year and *that* Lauren was far from perfect, but whatever.

We never truly understood why she felt she needed to put on pre-tenses, for us especially, we knew behind that good girl mask was a mustang begging to be freed, to get away from her jackass of a husband. Trent wasn't any better than Desmond, Olivia's husband. Believe it or not, they were cut from the same cloth. Only difference was Desmond at least kept a hustle.

Most of the time, admittedly these side-hustles weren't long-lasting, but it was better effort than we've ever seen from Trent. I've never been a fan of a man having a side hustle, but no main hustle? Where's the main hustle, aka day job? Just no. Olivia was a better woman than me.

At least Desmond was not sitting around like Trent, just reliving his glory days of being an 'almost' NFL player. Was I being too judgy and hard on Trent? Possibly. I sipped my drink as I slow-winded against Tate, to Rihanna's hit song *Only Girl (in the world)*. We were in our own bubble. Floating on celestial stardust and a deepening desire. In his arms, under the spell of his masculine grip, I was drifting between nirvana and euphoria.

His eyes traveled down to mine.

Beneath his gaze I felt like a goddess. An enchantress. Completely free to explore the realms of my seduction. My gaze wandered to his lips. They looked supple, moist, aching for me to capture them between mine.

"Do you see something you like?" he asked deeply.

"Oh yeah," I murmured.

I cuffed his face between my palms and pulled it down to mine. Ravaging his mouth and completely forgetting we were in public. Side effects of a lot of alcohol. Or simply the irresistible longing brewing to the surface. Either way I didn't care. The way his soft caramel skin felt rubbing against mine was insatiable. We stayed in this moment of bliss for minutes before coming up for air.

I swallowed, granting my lips some reprieve, but I wanted more. The caged yearning for him had kicked down the door that I had previously locked it behind. Our eyes remained on each other. Never wavering. We breathed in sync.

Time stood still until he raised his head.

He tapped my backside lightly to get my attention. "Ava, look."

"What?" I asked, turning around.

When I looked across the pool to my cabana, I saw Camille and Olivia arguing, arms flinging in all directions, again. *Dear God, what now?* I wondered as I regained my senses.

"Tate, I'll be right back."

I left the heavenly state I was in to go see what kind of hell these two were raising. Due to my level of inebriation, reading lips was out of the question. I didn't need to know what had been said to know that shit had finally hit the fan.

My feet carried me to the other side as fast as they could. The instant I arrived, I knew it was some stupid stuff not meant to be aired in public. The cameraman had the camera on them as they bickered.

"Camille, you are a toxic individual," Olivia shouted. "You're just jealous I'm on television and not you. Don't be mad at me because you couldn't cut it and your so-called acting attempt fizzled before it got started!"

"Ha...acting! You call this acting?" Camille mocked. "This isn't acting, this is a train wreck. And don't worry about my failed acting career. You need to be worried about your cheating-ass husband!"

My eyes almost jumped out their sockets. Whoa! She went there.

"Hold up, hold up," I quickly interjected. "Wait a damn minute. Camille, you know you're wrong as hell for spilling that on camera. You knew she didn't want that on film." I threw up my hands like a referee but it was too late, the hateful point had been scored.

"Go to hell, Ava!" she snapped back. "You have a lot of nerve. Who do you think you are chastising me? You brought us here for some *girls' weekend*, but instead of hanging with your girls, you've been over there windin' and grindin' on Tate for the past few hours!"

The contempt in her tone was razor sharp. Camille was angry and nothing any of us had done had made her that way. She had some personal issues going on and she was deflecting. I know I didn't deserve this wrath, from her of all people.

"What did I miss?" Lauren asked, returning with a mimosa in her hand and shock on her face. "Camille? Olivia? What's going on?"

Olivia turned towards her. "Nothing's going on. Nothing except Camille can't handle someone other than her being the center of attention."

Camille scowled at her insult.

"First of all, nobody cares about you being some D-list star of a lil' reality show that's going to flop," Camille smirked maliciously. "Family Values my ass. Since when? Not the Evergreens that I know. This whole idea is a joke."

I stood with my mouth hung agape. Lauren too. We were both speechless. Caught off guard by what was happening. Insanely thrown at the fact Camille was purposefully sabotaging Olivia's show. And the nastiness, to her face, was next level. It had been years since we argued at this low level, like, before graduation. We prided ourselves as a clique on being a bit 'bad and bougie', and this right here, not bougie at all, not cool.

"Again I ask, what show?" Lauren asked again. How she was still oblivious to the camera crew was beyond understanding, but whatever. Lauren had a weird way of only seeing what she wanted to see, with her dear hubby Trent being exhibit A.

"Ugh, girl, keep up" Camille groaned, irritated by Lauren's inquiry. "Olivia has some new show about her and her dysfunctional family. Did you not peep all these camera people following her around? Earth to Lauren!"

My brain wasn't processing what was happening fast enough. The words were at the tip of my tongue, but they wouldn't come out. I was frozen. Stuck in this daze. The only body part not frozen were my eyeballs as they kept moving rapidly trying to grasp how they'd gotten here. I mean, I could guess, considering Camille was tripping earlier, but I didn't want to assume that she kicked the drama off.

"Wait, Liv...you're on television?" Lauren asked like there wasn't an intense argument occurring. "Is that why the cameras are here? Huh, I thought it was Ava recording for her business, that blog or whatever she's doing."

I lowered my head, slowly shaking it at how bad her timing was right now. Lauren managed to appear naive and shade my very thriving company all at the same time. Blog? Really. She knows that a simple blog could never. But this was not the time to delve into Olivia's newest endeavors. She was late to the party, and we'd fill her in later. Dirty laundry was being aired and it needed to stop. Now.

"Who cares!" Olivia blurted out, at her level ten, outdoor voice.

I was outdone. This was exactly why The Alexander was hesitant about letting her into their five star establishment with cameras. This right here. Thankfully, we had dodged that bullet, because who knows if Tate would even be speaking to me if this had gone down in The Alexander.

"Olivia, I need you to lower your voice. You're drawing attention." I pointed to the plethora of eyes and camera phones recording us. "This, whatever this is, can be handled back at the villa." If I hadn't been so deeply bronzed and sun-kissed, I'm sure my face would have been red from embarrassment, and well, frankly anger at how my birthday trip was devolving into madness.

Camille bent her head back and cackled. She sounded louder than ever and absolutely unhinged. I considered loading the Better Help app on my phone and sticking it in her face, as she needed immediate professional help. Therapy, girl, look into it. *(Oops, I had recently been told the same thing. That paramedic wasn't wrong, if I'm honest.)*

"Good old Ava to the rescue. You know, you pretend to be such a loyal friend to us all. 'Oh I've missed you all. Oh come celebrate my birthday and let's be close again.' When in reality, you aren't any better than any of the other girls." Camille rolled her eyes hard.

I lifted a brow at her insinuation. Brushing past Lauren, I closed the gap between us, ensuring she could hear me loud and clear. I scowled at her as I looked her squarely in her eyes.

"Let me make one thing clear, I'm not Olivia, nor am I anybody else you must have me confused with. I know you. And I know that *you* know that I'm not the one to play with. Now unless you want me to put all your business on front street, and I do mean *all of it*, you better chill the hell out."

I glared at her. She did the same. I didn't care as long as she knew I wasn't playing with her. I had no qualms about blowing up her spot. The only role I played in this secret was not being forthcoming. But that was only to remain neutral. However, I had no problem choosing a side today.

We stood face-to-face for a few minutes longer until someone from the resort appeared.

"Excuse me," the older man said. He looked very dignified in a suit and tie that was clearly custom, but also he wore a badge and gave off strong authoritarian vibes.

I broke our stare to give him my attention.

"Yes," I answered.

"Are you Miss Richards?" he inquired.

"I am."

"I'm sorry, but I'm going to have to ask you and your guests to leave the premises. Unfortunately, we've received a few complaints regarding a loud disturbance from your section."

This is beyond ghetto.

I was fuming. Causing a disturbance was one thing, being put out was something totally different. Somehow I was feeling more and more like a reality tv star than I wanted to.

"I apologize, Mr…"

"Suarez," he answered.

"Mr. Suarez, I apologize for my friends. But I assure you the situation is now under control. If we could just consider this a warning, there won't be any more issues," I attempted to persuade him.

His lips folded into a tight smile. I knew what that meant even before he opened his mouth. That rigid smile and eyes without even a hint of empathy indicated that this conversation was over.

The two of them had acted a complete fool…and on camera at that! There was no way he was giving us a pass. I silently accepted this defeat and nodded, acknowledging that I understood the predicament he'd been put in.

Everyone was staring and allowing us to stay was bad for business. The other customers, spending thousands per night, were not here for it and I couldn't blame them. I stepped up onto the deck to retrieve my belongings so we could leave. I didn't even bother saying anything to the girls, since nothing polite would have left my lips.

If they didn't read between the lines, they'd be escorted out. I'm sure Ian might not mind, but I was disgusted by all of their shenanigans. In the back of my mind, I wondered what Tate must be thinking, but I decided that I certainly had bigger fish to fry back at the villa, this had to be sorted once and for all.

"Ava," Olivia started to plead.

"Save it. I don't want to hear it," I retorted, storming out.

18

Chapter Eighteen: Reservoir of Truths

I gazed out the window. The breeze from the ceiling fan blew gently over the sheer curtains. I exhaled softly, gradually releasing the madness of what occurred last night from my tightly wound body. After the pool party, the arguing continued in the villa. More hurtful things were said. Feelings were trampled upon. All of it caught on camera. This was certainly not the vacation trip I envisioned when I invited them.

I should've brought Jade instead. Now I could fully understand why my cousin and bestie refused to have anything to do with these girls.

I closed my eyes again, tightly this time, wishing last night was just a dream. But it wasn't. It was all too real. A real nightmare. I had hoped we would reconnect. Find our way back to being the best of friends again, but that didn't seem plausible anymore. Too much time had passed, and we'd all grown apart, to different degrees, but we just weren't the same fun crew we used to be, that much was certain.

Tate pulled me closer to him to close the small gap that formed between us. His cozy body next to mine was the perfect way to wake up after a night like that. I willingly complied with his silent summons, nestling my body within the natural curve our silhouettes had carved out.

"Mmmm..." he moaned in my ear. "Good morning, beautiful."

I smiled against the fluffy pillow. His compliments would never get old. Neither would the scent of him. I was enjoying how my skin and clothing were saturated with it. His warmth pressed up against mine was something I'd enjoy waking up to every morning happily.

"Good morning."

I rolled over to face him. Morning breath and all. His eyes looked quite different in the early morning light. From this close angle, I was able to see the outer ring of hazel that circled his whiskey-colored irises. The facial hair that surrounded the lips I enjoyed kissing last night glistened. Tate was truly a work of art.

I lifted my hand to trace my fingers over his thick, lush eyebrows. They were prickly, yet soft. I caressed his smooth butterscotch caramel skin. There was something to be said about a man who was well-groomed and practiced good skin care techniques.

Leaning forward, I gently pressed my lips against his, savoring his taste yet again. Shortly following the pool party debacle, he called me to check on me. When I told him things had gone from bad to worse, he immediately invited me to his place to rescue me from the chaos.

I happily obliged.

Being abruptly tossed out of the pool party, I missed the opportunity to say goodbye. The second-hand embarrassment forced me to rush out. I parted my lips, and our tongues dueled again, this time better than the last. I eased my leg over his and pressed my pelvis against him. Heat surged through my lower region the further his hand crept up my shirt.

I was still fully dressed from last night.

All we had done was talk and swap stories. He told me more about him and what he did for a living and vice versa. We switched between talking and touching. Laughing and feeling each other up like two teenagers toddling between second and third base. There was no pressure. Only intimacy. Then we eventually fell asleep.

And I enjoyed it.

Falling asleep with an attractive man without worrying about being fondled or taken advantage of in the middle of the night was a rarity. I certainly didn't make a habit of sleepovers with strangers, but there was something truly special about Tate. Once I arrived at his place, the night had been perfect, safe and still highly erotic. He made room for the organic chemistry between us to grow even more.

I enveloped his lips with mine. Moving them slowly, sensually, against his. There was a certain ebb and flow to our kissing. Give and take. Surrender and conquer. Sometimes it was him. Other times it was me. Every time, satisfaction was guaranteed.

He eased his lips away from mine, and began stroking his thumb across my bottom lip. *Even his subtle touches had purpose.* I teased with my tongue, hoping to excite him and intrigue him the way he had me.

"Mmm," he moaned.

I twirled my tongue around, seductively teasing him. Our eyes locked into each others eyes, and possibly souls. I basked in this moment.

Freeing his thumb, I recaptured his lips with mine. We only had two more days together and I was starting to feel separation anxiety. I had never felt this way about anyone before. Not even Cameron. *(Since meeting Tate, in a matter of days, Cameron had quickly become a distant memory, with me even forgetting to tell the girls when we were at dinner the other night. Cameron who?)*

Was this how people felt when they met their soulmates? Was this love at first sight?

"You have beautiful eyes," he said.

I nodded, coyly smiling at his flattering words. "Yours are quite fascinating to stare into as well."

His dimple revealed itself as his cheeks rose. Then he placed a kiss on my forehead. A simple reaction to making him blush.

"What are you getting into today?" he asked.

"Not sure. Right about now, I'm ready to go back to LA, because this birthday party week didn't work out as planned."

"No, you can't do that, Ava. Not before you let me take you on a proper date tomorrow."

"A date? What kind of date?" Inside, my heart was fluttering, doing jumping jacks and somersaults. The good kind, not the panic attack kind that I dreaded. This was the confirmation I needed, that Tate was seeing me in the same way I viewed him. Promising.

"You'll see. Go deal with your friends, sort everything out, I'll send you the details later on. Check your phone before bed tonight, yeah?"

I smiled. "Are you really not going to tell me what we're doing tomorrow?"

He shook his head.

"Can you at least tell me what I should wear?" I asked, hoping to get him to give me some kind of clue.

"Wear something that makes you feel beautiful. And comfy. I'll provide the rest." Tate stated, with his confidence on full display again. Hmm. That's the attitude I like, Tate. Do that.

"Fine...be that way. Keep your secrets." I pretended to pout.

He chortled and it was the most joyful sound I'd ever heard a man release. "You're very cute when you pout, you know."

"Yeah, yeah." I rolled over to get up. "There's still time to get it out of you."

"I'm resolute. Solid as a rock. Nothing is cracking this vault." Tate made a face that I imagined he used in the kitchen when he was barking orders to his sous chefs.

"It seems I failed to tell you I'm quite the accomplished negotiator." He walked over to my side of the bed.

Pulling me closer to him, he wrapped his arms around my waist. "Is that so?" he asked, grinning. "Then I'm sure you know in order to negotiate, you must have something to negotiate with. What are you looking to barter with?"

My fingers crawled up his shirt as I taunted his skin.

I answered, "Depends."

"On..." He arched his eyebrow inquisitively.

I stood on my toes. "I'll tell you tomorrow."

* * *

The instant I entered the villa, I felt the chilly atmosphere. A pin could fall and it would be heard throughout the house. I started to call out for the ladies to meet up in the grand foyer, but decided I'd take a shower first. I was still on a romantic high from spending the night and this morning with Tate. I didn't want it ruined just yet. I took off my sandals, then headed towards my bedroom.

"Ava?" I heard Lauren call out.

Damn, I was so close.

I turned around slowly to see her standing in the doorway, holding a mug of tea. She must've been on the patio when I came in. "Good morning, Lauren. Where's everyone at this morning?"

"Not sure. I saw Olivia leave earlier, followed by an entire camera crew. Which speaking of...what's that all about?"

"Long story," I nonchalantly shrugged off the invitation to dwell on the Olivia and Camille drama. I mean, at this point, those two had carved out an entire episode for themselves in what was meant to be *my* birthday celebration. Not bitter, just disappointed. I went directly to the Keurig to brew myself a cup, in case we ended up in a full on conversation about recent events, I would need a coffee and a banana bread muffin at least.

"But what's up? You look like you have a lot on your mind."

She crossed her arms, squeezing her biceps, and gave me a slight nod. The look on her face implied it was something serious. I wasn't a mind reader, though Lauren's thoughts had settled on her face. And I had a feeling I knew what they were regarding.

"I do. Do you have a moment? I wanted to talk for a second," she said softly.

I inhaled deeply.

Truthfully speaking, I wanted to shower and lay across the bed, and daydream about Tate and all of the 'what if's. What if we had? I was proud of my self-restraint, but the what if factor was super intense right now, and Tate was almost all I could think about this morning.

Yesterday's drama was draining and I wasn't ready to revisit what happened, even though she wasn't at fault and wasn't even a part of what went down. I hadn't forgotten about our conversation yesterday in lieu of the pool party fiasco. My intention was to address it, I just needed time to collect my thoughts.

"May I ask what about?"

"Us," she replied.

Sooner definitely came faster than later. Bobbing my head at her request, I started moving closer to her. Now was probably a better time anyway since everyone else was off doing their own thing and we were able to speak freely in case things got heated, which I was sure they would, because neither of us were ever capable of biting our tongues. As an Aries, I could be fun and fiery, but nobody commits to long-winded lectures, Ted talks, like my Taurus sister Lauren. When Lauren wants "to talk" brace yourself. I knew that she could literally say anything right now. Ugh!

I followed her out of the sliding glass door and onto the deck. In a matter of minutes, our feet were in the sand as we walked down to the beach. We had our privacy to speak freely, because the villa was on the more remote side of the resort and there was not a lot of foot traffic.

"Did you want to sit, or talk and walk?" I asked her.

"Either is fine."

I'd rather walk since I didn't get a chance to enjoy the sunrise this morning. Walking would also help keep my heart rate steady. I found that difficult conversations were usually easier if you walked side by side, rather than sit in a face to face confrontational position.

Sometimes if I had to have a hard talk with one of my employees, I would suggest a walk to get coffee. Of course, eventually the staff would catch on and dread walking anywhere with me, so it's not an entirely foolproof method.

Of course, Lauren wasn't my employee, she was supposed to be one of my girls, a best friend for life.

"Let's walk then," I suggested. "What's on your mind?"

"Why did you invite me, Ava?" she came right out and asked. "We haven't talked in close to what? More than ten years? What made you decide to reach out now?"

That's a fair question, I thought. I should have been more clear in the email. I see I didn't communicate as clearly as I thought I did, apparently.

"I invited you, Lauren, because I missed you. The way things ended with our friendship, I didn't like it, and I felt with our history, things shouldn't have gone down like that. You completely shut me out."

Lauren stopped in her tracks and faced me. So much for being non-confrontational.

"Are you serious right now?" She looked perturbed by my response. "Is that how you're going to start this off—pointing the finger at me?"

I folded my arms.

"Is that not what happened?" I questioned. I wanted to remain sincere and focused on the point at hand.

"Yes, but we both know that's not the entire story. You're only addressing my reaction to your action, or have you forgotten that part?"

"Lauren, I didn't forget anything." A small snort escaped, against my will.

"Then how can you stand here and say it's my fault?"

I sighed then reiterated, "I didn't say it was your fault. I simply stated you shut me out. Is that not a fact?"

"Fine," she said sharply. "You didn't say it was my fault, but you certainly *implied* that it was."

I rubbed my temple, feeling frustration build, and possibly my temper rising.

This is exactly why I didn't want to do this right now. I hadn't gotten all of my angst from last night out and having this discussion with bitterness still in my system was a bad idea. But had I said, 'let's talk later,' then being a control freak would've been thrown up in my face. It was their go-to for everything Ava-related.

Should I really have to apologize for being in control of things, when we have some clear examples of what happens when you lose control? Stop it, Ava! This is the judgy-ness that everyone is so sick of, do better!

"Lauren, I never meant to hurt you. You have to know that was not the intention at all behind it."

"Oh really? Then how else would you describe not showing up to my wedding? We were best friends Ava, you were my maid of honor for heaven's sake, what did you think not showing up *on my wedding day* would do to us?"

Her voice cracked as her volume increased. The evidence of hurt she felt was apparent. But I had my reasons. Aside from the fact that I felt like she was throwing her life away, Trent wasn't worthy of her. That's ultimately what it boiled down to.

"Showing up would've meant that I thought what you were doing was in your best interest, and it wasn't."

"Humph," she shook her head, smirking. "You have a lot of damn nerve, you know that. The audacity you walk around with is immeasurable. I–I–I...I can't even believe you just said that."

She interlocked her fingers then placed her hands on top of her head. The stuck look on her face resembled complete shock and astonishment. Nevertheless, it was the truth. Trent was then what we now call a F-boy. And he never respected her or her friends for that matter.

"I didn't want it to come out like that. I mean..." I lowered my head to collect my thoughts. "What I meant was, Lauren, you were too good for him. I can't speak on what kind of person he is now, but who he was then... he didn't deserve to have you on his arm."

Lauren moved her hands down to place them on her hips. I saw her famously funky attitude creeping to the surface, knowing that this was about to get a lot worse before it got better. I blamed myself for this. All I had to do was go to the wedding, pretend like nothing had ever happened, and put on a fake smile. But I didn't.

I couldn't.

Perhaps if I was a fake friend, maybe. However, there was no way I could stand beside her and smile and nod in agreement, while he looked her dead in her eyes and lied to her in front of God and everyone else.

"You know, Ava, I know you believe you can control every aspect of your life, and others, but reality check, you can't. No one is perfect. And your idea of a 'perfect man' is unrealistic. They're all flawed."

If only I had a mirror right now. Girl, you need to see yourself saying this. I stared at her, astounded at the mere fact she let that fly out of her mouth. For as long as we had been friends, she'd been obsessed with perfection. To her own detriment might I add. Now here she was telling me I was naive for having unrealistic expectations for men, when she obviously had none.

"I shouldn't be surprised if you believe that," I blurted out.

She scoffed. "And what the hell is that supposed to mean?"

"It means you're standing here telling me not to have standards for men when you clearly don't have any yourself. And instead of you trying to create a happy life, or actually find a good man, you'd rather put on airs."

I bit down on my lip. The words leaving my lips sounded much worse than how they had in my head. Lauren's eyes welled up with tears and I knew that I had taken it too far, and was now bordering on mean. She only cried when she was truly angry.

I held up my hand.

"Lauren, wait. That could've come out, should've come out differently. Let's rewind, because I didn't come out here to argue. I'll start from the beginning. You asked me why I invited you and the truth is, I wanted us to clear the air and start over. In the spirit of doing that, I owe you the truth and transparency."

I took a deep breath. A shroud of hesitation covered me. Not because I was afraid to speak the truth, that was never really a problem for me. I was honestly worried that she *still* wasn't ready to hear it. We'd been down this road before. Several times to be exact. And it always ended the same way.

"The reason I didn't come to your wedding was because I couldn't stand there and listen to Trent lie to your face, knowing he'd made several advances at me. Along with other women around campus. As much as I wanted to be there for you, it hurt me to watch you make a mistake like that. I believed that he was only marrying you to ensure he didn't pass up a comfortable lifestyle if his football aspirations fell by the wayside. He didn't want to lose you, that's true, but for the wrong reasons."

Her eyes widened at my confession. She stood silent, taking it all in. Her lips tightened as she pressed them together. The eerie silence floated between us for a few minutes before she finally exhaled.

"Just to be sure I heard you correctly, you're telling me that you, my best friend, didn't show up to my wedding because my husband hit on you? Is that what you're telling me?"

"Lauren..."

She held her hand up, and shifted her weight towards me, edging a bit too close to my face for my liking. "No, ma'am. Answer the damn question."

"Yes, I didn't show up because Trent had been cheating on you, was still cheating on you when you married him, and tried to get me into bed."

She mocked me by raising her eyebrows sky-high and giving me a stare that doubled down and frankly, sent a slight chill over me.

"Or is it that you were *jealous*?"

I jerked my head back, utterly offended by her accusation. This was exactly why people kept their mouths closed in situations like this. It was a lose-lose situation for the messenger.

I held up my finger like the saints do when trying to slide between the pews and clean out of church.

"Let's be clear about something. I don't have a jealous bone in my body. Nor have I ever been jealous of any of you. But let's not stand here and pretend what I'm saying to you is foreign. You and I both know we've had several conversations where you've cried on my shoulder about Trent. Remember now, you had me riding with you past his dorm, calling him privately to see if he answers, etcetera, etcetera. The only new twist to this is that he finally got comfortable enough to dabble in your backyard, hitting on your own closest friends and it was very awful, Lauren." I had to make it plain if we were ever going to find a resolution, right?

Lauren looked down at her pedicured toes and seemed to take in the fact that she may have some culpability in this sour situation as well.

"Then why didn't you say anything? Why now?"

"Girl, how many times have the three of us come and talked to you about the rumors we heard around campus?" I paused for effect. "Huh, Lauren? I won't bother mentioning his greatest heartbreak hits because you know *all* of them. You heard what you wanted to hear. I don't know if you were trying to hold on in the event he made it to the league or what, but please don't act like you have amnesia."

"Telling me he hit on you would've made a difference, Ava."

"No it wouldn't have," I stated bluntly. "Now if we're being honest, let's keep it all the way real. Nothing any of us said would've changed anything. You married him knowing what we all knew, Lauren! We knew he had you wrapped around his finger. I realized then that I couldn't compete with pillow talk. He can be a charmer, he had already won you over. You were headed down that aisle come hell or highwater. Therefore, I bowed out."

"No, you took the cowardly way out." Lauren was stonefaced.

"That's your opinion and you're entitled to it. But I didn't want to ruin your wedding day, so I made the decision to forego attending. Afterwards, I tried to explain, but you blew a gasket, and things were left unsaid."

She turned her back to me.

I exhaled loudly, almost groaning, and releasing the pinned-up animosity I'd been carrying all these years.

"Lauren, I'm sorry. I should've said that years ago, but I am sorry, truly. What's done is done, and I can't change what happened, but I can apologize for my part in it. In hindsight, I should've handled the situation differently. I guess fear got the best of me. I played that scenario over in my head several times, and it always ended with you choosing him over your friends. So, to keep that from happening, I made the decision for you. It was the wrong decision, I see that now, but that's where my head was. In retrospect, I didn't want the agony of you pushing me away, but it happened anyway," I admitted.

She turned back around, tears running down her cheek. My eyes began to well up with fresh tears along with hers. It had taken me, like what, nearly fifteen years to say that. Fifteen years of regret, of saltiness, of being pissed off at her for doing what I knew she would do, but shouldn't have, in my opinion. But now, in my wisdom at forty, I see that it was just my opinion. *Who am I, to tell her what makes her happy?*

"I wish you would have trusted me enough, trusted in our friendship, our bond to know that I would have believed you, had you told me. Ava! I wish you had told me! *Instead you decided for me* because that's what you do, Ava. You've always done that. You predict how people are going to react to something and make decisions accordingly. I know that has panned out really well for you career wise, but you can't treat people like they're chess pieces to be moved around."

Her words echoed in my ears, floated around inside my head, clawed their way down deep into my consciousness. It was wrong not to tell the truth, and this is why we are here today. I hated this outcome.

"You're right, and I'm sorry," I acknowledged.

She gave me a caring smile.

"I'm sorry too. I should've allowed you the opportunity to explain yourself, I owed you that much."

We stood in silence for a moment too long, and that quickly became uncomfortable, but it was necessary to feel all the feelings to get past this.

I returned a small, quiet smile. "All is forgiven."

Lauren stopped close to me and embraced me.

"I missed you," she professed.

I wrapped my arms around her, hoping we have really resolved this once and for all, and then gently inhaling the relief I felt.

"I missed you too, friend."

19

Chapter Nineteen: Heart Riots

I woke up from my nap rejuvenated.

After returning from my long walk and conversation with Lauren, I needed rest. I was exhausted—mentally, emotionally, and physically. I hadn't gotten much sleep at Tate's place due to us being up so late into the night, chatting and goofing off. Having that hard talk with Lauren drained me even more. But I was really glad that, at last, Lauren and I had finally cleared the air. This was the sole reason I had invited all of them, for our collective resolution and peace of mind.

I still needed to have a conversation with Camille and Olivia. Only I wasn't sure I wanted to proceed now. Not with Camille anyway. Just knowing she might still be up to the same ole, same ole left me depleted. In light of her antics on this trip, I had no choice but to question whether or not our friendship was worth saving, or if I wanted to cut the cord on her toxicity and go about my business.

Was she still creeping behind Olivia's back? We suspect so. And she'd done it in the past, but somehow in our youth and inexperience it seemed we had just 'chalked it up to the game.'

Trouble is, this is now forty. Game time has been over. Salvaging a relationship with someone who didn't have a loyal bone in their body wasn't all that appealing. I had never been naive enough to think that she could do it to her, but not to me.

As far as I knew, she hadn't done it to me, or Lauren. Still, that didn't mean that if the right circumstances presented themselves, she wouldn't try it. My thoughts went back to how she was ogling Tate the other night. Anyone with eyes could see the way we were staring at each other. Hell, anyone with a pulse could feel the heat steaming off us. Why she thought he was available and fair game left me scratching my head.

Knock. Knock. Knock.

I rolled over to the light tapping on my door. I barely wanted to get out of this luxurious bed; between the high thread count sheets and the down feather bed, it felt like drifting on a cloud in heaven. Did I really want to be bothered? No.

"Come in," I said loudly.

Olivia peeked her head in. Her face was fully made up. The long hair she let hang the entire trip was pulled into a long French braid along the side of her head. She looked youthful. Innocent. Striking, even. I should have told her out loud, been more free with my compliments, but I was still in a fog of emotion from earlier.

I asked, "Where are you headed?"

"Dinner, silly. That's why I came to check on you. You slept the day away. I figured you didn't want to sleep the night away too."

I reached for my phone.

There was no way I slept the whole day away. I picked up my phone and saw it read 6:30 p.m. *Damn,* I thought. I had slept the day away. Since it was still light outside, I didn't think it was so late into evening. Time played tricks on you during the summer, and especially on vacation, it became so slippery.

"I'm getting up," I told her. I tossed the cover off and swung my legs over the side of the bed, and the cool of the tile floor shocked me further awake. "I took a shower already, so I just need to do a light beat and my hair."

"Hey, it's your birthday trip," she stated. "Whenever you get ready, you're ready."

How sweet. I smiled at her.

"Thanks, Liv, but I made reservations for us for eight. I'll be ready in an hour at the latest."

"Cool beans. I'll let the others know. See you when you get done."

I nodded and did a brisk walk to the closet. Originally I planned to wear my cream, strapless jumpsuit, but I decided to save that for my date with Tate. Wherever we were going. I combed through the many outfits that I packed, shuffling hangers back and forth, until I settled on the dainty magenta dress I had brought.

I loved everything about this dress. It was sexy, ultra-feminine, and eye-catching. The shoe-string spaghetti straps highlighted my shoulders and collarbone exquisitely, adding to the allure of the deep v-cut in front and back. The layers of lace ruffles rested on sheer silk, joining the feminine and eye-catching aspects beautifully.

The strappy gold sandals and clutch I brought were the perfect accessories. I didn't feel like doing too much to my hair, so I figured I'd throw it into a high bun, and with my large gold hoops, I'd be ready to go.

Perfect!

* * *

"To friendship," I said, raising my champagne glass to toast. "I appreciate all of you coming to celebrate my big 4-0 with me. I really do. It means a lot."

"Cheers," Olivia chimed in, clinking her glass against the others.

We were eating dinner together, finally. It only took a decade of no one talking, multiple emails, me paying for it and three spontaneous pop ups scattered over seven days for it to happen. But it did happen at last, and I felt grateful. Lauren and I had made amends and it felt good to sit next to her without the tension I sensed when she first arrived. Camille was behaving, so for now I was satisfied. Olivia appeared to be in better spirits, despite the crying session I heard her having earlier before I eventually fell asleep.

She wasn't aware that I could hear her since she assumed I was asleep, but I did. Instinctively, I almost got up to check on her, then decided to let her be. She needed this time with herself. The private space to cleanse her soul alone. If she sought out solace, she knew where I was.

Olivia immediately downed her champagne and reached for the bottle to refill her glass. Camille's annoyance for Liv's excessive drinking didn't get past me. If it were genuine concern, I would understand, but it wasn't. I didn't know what it was, but these past few days, she seemed so irritated by Olivia. Me too, at times. But more so Camille was giving major hating vibes, and that was disturbing.

"Liv," Lauren cut through the brief silence. "Tell me about this show you're on. I feel like I'm the only one who doesn't know what's going on."

Olivia perked up at Lauren's interest in her newest endeavor.

"Well, it's a cable network show, produced by an Emmy award winner, and it centers on my crazy life, so its all about me, Desmond, and the kids," she bragged. "Four years ago, I started filming some of our family moments and posted them to Instagram. People loved them! There'd be all kinds of comments like, '*they love our family dynamics, our family is beautiful, we're hilarious,*' stuff like that. When I saw the responses and all of the likes, I knew we might have something here, so I recorded more. After about three or four months of doing that, someone suggested that we start a YouTube channel. I'd considered it, but dismissed it. But it came up again and again, so I ran it by Desmond. He'd heard how you could monetize being on YouTube, so he was fully onboard with it."

Of course he was.

Lauren nodded knowingly. "Okay, so how did you get the show, on cable tv?" She was fully vested now. And so was I, particularly considering that Olivia hadn't divulged any of these details the entire time she'd been here.

"We got the show because of our YouTube channel actually," she replied confidently. "It garnered so much attention, a network reached out to us about doing a show. Since I had done a few guest appearances, as a 'friend of' on another local reality show, the network recognized me from there. And well, the rest is history."

"Wow, Liv, I'm happy for you," Lauren congratulated her. "I'm glad to see you've found your rhythm, and with your family nonetheless."

Olivia took a sip of her champagne.

"Thanks," she said with a hint of reluctance. I wasn't sure if anyone else had caught onto it or not, but I had. "Though, I'm not sure how everything is going to unfold once I get back home."

Confusion graced all of our faces.

"What do you mean?" I asked. This was the first time she seemed bummed out about the show. When she first arrived she damn near twisted my arm to let them stay, now she wasn't sure if she wanted to continue with filming. I refrained from making a comment since I was always the one painted as the villain. "You were just so excited about it."

"Right, what gives?" Lauren asked.

Olivia sighed heavily before finishing off another drink. She grabbed the Veuve bottle by the neck and filled her glass to the brim, again. I was beginning to worry about her. I knew we all had ways of dealing with issues and coping with the vices that somehow managed to attach to us during hard times. However, her drinking had been a bit extreme since she'd been here.

We weren't twenty-something young women anymore. Everyone with the exception of Lauren was forty now. Alcohol hit differently at this age. The liver was not so forgiving. The headaches lasted longer, and the sleep became tumultuous after too many drinks. Did she not see the sabotage of it all? I felt more sure now that for Olivia, drinking had become a convenient numbing mechanism, so that she could avoid acknowledging the very truths we were here to sort out.

"I'm asking Desmond for a divorce when I get back," she revealed. Aha! There it is.

Lauren had the same reaction that I had the other night when Olivia admitted she felt he was cheating in their marriage. I was equally surprised, seeing as though I didn't know things had escalated since then. She'd gone from *suspecting* an affair, to outright divorce in seventy-two hours.

What happened? I sipped my drink as we all waited for her to elaborate. Olivia took a couple of gulps as if this liquid would give her the courage to speak her mind. The camera crew members sat behind her, faces riddled with bewilderment, waiting for the same reactions as we were. I rested my palm on her hand as a show of moral support. The two of us hadn't quite cleared the air completely, but that didn't mean I wasn't going to be here for her.

"Marriage is hard," Olivia finally said. "Really hard. No one tells you *how hard,* or at least you don't fully believe them. I'm not sure which it was for me." She shook her head gradually from side-to-side to wrangle her budding emotions. "Maybe I thought the fiery love we shared was enough to withstand anything that blew our way, good or

175

bad. I'm now realizing that love just isn't enough- especially if it's built on a lie."

The table grew quiet as Olivia poured her heart out. I was eternally grateful I had requested a private room this time around. And I wondered if that's why she felt comfortable enough to unleash everything. I motioned to dismiss the camera people again, but she stopped me.

"Olivia," Lauren said in the most endearing tone I'd ever heard her speak. "Marriage is hard. Hard as hell. Some days you adore your husband. Others, you want to punch him in the face. Yet, you still love him," she told her, glancing at me. But I could neither confirm, nor deny. Cameron and I had never made it down the aisle, so what did I know?

Lauren carried on with the comforting words, "Over the years I've learned that marriage is made up of a variety of layers. Yes, love is one of them, but so is respect, trust, loyalty, and friendship. You need all of them. I won't try to sway you since I'm not privy to the ins and outs of your marriage; however, I will say, please take some time to think about this." She paused and looked up as if requesting help from above to make her case. "You've invested time, money, and pieces of yourself into this relationship. None of which you can get back. Therefore, before you take this huge leap, ask yourself—*have I done everything I can to make this work? Is this worth saving?*"

Lauren's advice was appropriate. Considering she was the only other married person in our friend group, she was the perfect one to respond. I'd had relationships, but not a marriage. Cameron and I shared something of a life together, we had been semi-serious, but just not in a permanent aspect. Marriage was something different altogether. An arena I was entirely unfamiliar with. Immediately I thought of last night with Tate, and how he made me feel. For a split second, I imagined what the future could hold for us, but I decided not to go there.

"I hear you, Lauren, but honestly, it's that I feel trapped. I have these amazing kids that I love with all of my heart, and I don't want to hurt them, much less raise them alone without their dad, so I deal with whatever happens for that reason."

I cringed internally at her response. On the outside, Olivia was this gorgeous woman who could walk a runway with the best of them. However, on the inside, she seemed to still be this fragile little girl unsure of her beauty or potential.

"I get that. Girl, hell, I always tell Trent if he ever thinks he's leaving me with these kids, he has another thing coming. If anything, they're going with him. Just bring them to me on the weekends." She joked around to lighten the mood. We tried to chuckle, but we all knew that she would never let her kids go that easily, and we understood Olivia's pain as well. "Seriously though, marriage and parenting are hard on their own. Being a wife and then a mom to a bunch of kiddos, yeah, it's a roller coaster of emotions and people on your damn nerves."

Olivia laughed loudly at her rant, obviously understanding her fully.

"To hell with that," Camille interjected. "If he's cheating then leave the bum! Why stay with someone who clearly doesn't want to be with you."

The glare I shot her pierced through her like daggers. Lauren shook her head, not the least bit surprised at Camille's 'go nuclear' advice. Camille shrugged off our disapproving reactions by finishing off the last sip of her glass.

"What?" she asked, annoyed by us staring at her. "Y'all can stare a hole in my head all you want. We all know once a cheater, always a cheater."

Is she for real right now? Of all the people?

I continued to stare at her in amazement. To think she'd done the unthinkable with Desmond and was trying to advise somebody. More and more I was taken aback by her brazen hypocrisy.

"Olivia," Lauren said. "Another piece of advice for you. Don't take marriage advice from non-married folks, or people who aren't even in a solid relationship." Incoming, Camille. Ouch.

"You don't know what I'm in, so mind your business, start there," Camille rebutted. "That's the problem now. Folks are always encouraging women to stay in broken marriages or toxic relationships. Girl, get out!"

I didn't bother acknowledging Camille any further, simply because I couldn't be responsible for what I said if I did. My eyes were focused on Olivia. Then the camera crew moved behind her to the guy sitting next to the camera man. He made a face at him, and I caught it. I'd wished she would let me excuse them from hearing this, it was so awkward for everyone at this point.

"Thanks, y'all. I appreciate the advice, all of it." She rubbed her finger underneath her lower lid to catch the tear before it fell. "Woo, okay, enough red table talk drama. Where's the check? It's time to go." She shook off her brief moment of heartache. "I'm ready to party now. We can turn up properly since the gang's back together again."

I cracked a half smile at her *gang's back together* reference. Mainly because I knew it was temporary. This reunion-slash-birthday bash had been a beautiful attempt, on my part, at resolution and reconciliation, if I may say so myself. But it was just that, an attempt *at best*. Like, how if you pull the trigger, without hitting your target, it can still be considered an attempt, and you can still be charged with a crime.

20

Chapter Twenty: Icarus

"*Another round of shots....Turn down for what!*"
Lil Jon shouted over the speakers as the whole club turned up. Olivia suggested we leave the resort and try out a local club. I was reluctant to go along with it, but with a production crew in tow, I realized that for the sake of her show, it was probably better to be out and about. Besides, we had all gone to the trouble of flying into Mexico, so we may as well see some authentic city life.

The neon fluorescent lights glowed throughout the club. Sweat-drenched bodies moved beneath them. Clouds of smoke, fragrances, and the smell of fried foods- shrimp taquitos, I guessed- saturated the thick air. Mango margaritas were flowing and for the past two hours, it felt like spring break in college all over again. This was the freest I'd ever felt. And it was exactly how I wanted to feel in this new chapter, this new decade of my life.

The past ten years had been filled to the brim with grind and hustle, at every opportunity. The next ten were going to be filled with living to the fullest. Living my best life. Living out my wildest dreams. Living with pure intention. My trip was coming to an end. Despite the handful of mishaps, overall it was a great trip. Clearing the air with Olivia was still needed, but I didn't want to make light of everything she had going on right now.

Dealing with an adulterous husband was enough. I would hold off until the very end of our trip so that we could at least enjoy the remainder without any hiccups or ill feelings. I looked around, and suddenly noticed that Olivia had totally disappeared. Should I be worried, and where were the others?

Camille was dirty dancing with some hot looking guy (despite her judgments of others doing the same), and meanwhile Lauren danced solo in the corner of the VIP section. Her moves suggested she was the star of her own telenovela, with all eyes on her, her hands gesturing crazily in the air and twirling about wildly, just like one might after unlimited tequila shots.

I scanned the crowd to search for Olivia.

She'd been drinking quite a bit and I didn't want her to do anything too rambunctious, that she'd be upset or ashamed about in the morning. Even though Desmond's despicable behavior was in question, I knew Olivia well enough to know she didn't want to be in the same boat as him. Regret had a way of making you feel much worse than the deed itself. My eyes perused the crowd until I spotted one of the camera guys.

Zeroing in on him, I looked closer to see that Olivia was fixed between them, peering over the chubbier one's arm as they showed her something on the screen. I was curious to know what they were showing her since they were huddled up in the corner rather than in VIP with the rest of us.

Olivia touched the screen as she pointed to something. I observed her body language, watching it shift from a relaxed stance to a more defensive one. Her shoulders broadened as her head slowly rose. The tension in my body became elevated. Olivia's eyes narrowed as her nostrils flared as she moved in our direction. I wanted to move, I really did, but my feet wouldn't budge.

I was transfixed by the fury in her face as I watched what was about to unfold.

Within seconds, Olivia had bolted from the other side of the club to where we were standing. My eyes were glued on her as she blew past me with the speed of lightning. Before I comprehended what was happening, Olivia snatched the glass Lauren was holding in her hand from her grasp, lunging its contents at Camille's face.

"You are so trifling!" Olivia yelled over the music. "I can't believe you could do this to me! How could you?"

Everyone including Camille stopped in their tracks to see what Olivia's outburst was all about. Blue liquid dripped down Camille's face as she stood stunned at Olivia tossing a whole drink at her.

"How could you? Of all the men in the world, you had to screw my husband?" she shouted, before launching at Camille. Knocked off balance, Camille fell backwards as Olivia jumped on top of her. One Louboutin heel flew up into the air, and an earring clinked and bounced across the floor. I blinked twice taking all of the shenanigans in. It appeared as if whatever she was looking at on that camera certainly did involve Camille and Desmond.

Camille had no idea Olivia even had a reality show, or was being filmed, so it was safe to say she wasn't aware that they had been filming Desmond either. Which made it even worse, because one would think he'd be looking out for Camille, not putting her in harm's way.

My body movements were halted as they tussled on the ground in front of me. The shock of it all had me frozen in place.

Olivia swung ferociously at Camille's face as she did her best to block the blows being delivered. I glanced over to see that Lauren was at a loss for words too. Her hand was still cupped as if her drink was still in it. I wanted to laugh almost as much as I wanted to cry, because it was all too absurd. This can not be real life.

Snapping out of my daze, I moved swiftly to break up the fight. By now, glasses had been knocked onto the floor, the crowd around us had grown, phones were pointed at them recording the latest 'sold to TMZ' video to be uploaded. I was embarrassed, but mostly angry. Angry that Camille had allowed herself to be put in this situation, and in turn putting the rest of us knee deep in this hot mess.

"I hate you, you are a piece of trash. What kind of friend does this to another!" she yelled, still wailing at Camille's head.

As I looked past the crowd, I saw security rushing towards us. We needed to break this up immediately before both of them ended up in a Mexican jail. I shook Lauren so she'd snap out of it and help me. "Lauren, snap out of it!" I shouted. "We need to go- now!"

Lauren nodded, indicating that she understood what I was saying to her. Bending over, she helped me pull Olivia off of Camille. Olivia continued kicking and screaming as Lauren held onto her while I got Camille off the ground. I had half of a mind to leave her down there, but we always abided by the rules; *we come together, we leave together.* No matter what. I extended my arm to Camille, helping her off the ground.

Her hair was wildly strewn over her head. Fresh scratches from Olivia's long nails bulged on top of her skin. The dress she had on was disheveled, barely covering her at this point. *She had this coming,* I thought, staring at her. A contemptuous smirk sat at the corner of my lips. I told her that payback was a bitch, and by the looks of her, karma had finally circled her block and rang her doorbell.

My empathy tank was empty.

I turned my back on her to check on Olivia.

Lauren was still trying to calm her down. Her heavy, labored breathing was a sign that adrenaline was still racing through her veins. Mascara stained her cheeks leaving evidence of her recent tears. Olivia was a wreck. And who wouldn't be after learning your so-called friend was the very same woman as the mistress you'd been stressing over.

Security finally pushed their way through the large crowd to see them standing in the opposing corners. Two bulky men that looked like they could very well be related to 'The Rock' and Floyd Mayweather approached us. They didn't have to utter a single word. Their large overpowering loftiness and ripped muscles spoke volumes.

It was time to go. Plain and simple.

I gave Lauren a hand signal to escort Olivia out first and I would follow with Camille behind me. Quickly, we vacated the club to avoid any legal actions being taken against us. I was thoroughly pissed at Camille for her role in this betrayal, and highly vexed at the camera crew for telling Olivia, here, on my trip, when they could've waited until she was alone. But then that wouldn't have created this meltdown moment.

This was exactly why I detested anything surrounding reality shows. Exploiting emotions for profit. That might sound weird considering I worked in media myself, but trust me, its not the same thing.

This was cruel. They lived for drama and did whatever was necessary to contrive it at the expense of someone else's reputation.

Once we were outside, Olivia made another run at Camille.

"You really played in my face and fed me all that bullshit! You told me to divorce my husband! And knowing you were the one sleeping with him!" she yelled.

I didn't hold an ounce of sympathy for Camille, and if we weren't in a different country, she'd be figuring out her own way home. I wasn't in the mood to referee them the whole way back to the resort.

"The uber should be here soon," Lauren informed me.

I nodded, confirming I heard her. There was nothing for me to say. This trip had been more disastrous than I anticipated. I expected some raw feelings being unleashed, but nothing to this degree. Nothing could have prepared me for this.

The two of them continued their screaming match.

"Aren't you going to say something?" Lauren asked me.

I shook my head. Nope, I was going to stay out of it. Any other time I inserted myself into *their* issues, I was being a control freak.

"Not a word," I stated plainly. "This has nothing to do with me." Never had the words *'boundaries'* and *'self care'* been more applicable.

We turned our attention back to the real-life soap opera that was playing out in front of us. The uber had pulled up just in time. I walked over to it and climbed in the front seat, waiting as Lauren ushered Olivia and Camille to the car.

I reached into my purse and pulled out a hundred-dollar bill.

"This will be your tip if you get us back to Costa Palmas as quickly as possible. And trust me when I say, you'll want to step on it."

"Si, Señora," he said, smiling at the money in my hand. After years of city life, I had learned how to properly incentivize at the right time, to keep things moving.

Everyone climbed into the car and the instant the door was closed, he stepped on it. The bickering continued the entire ride. He occasionally glanced at me, silently acknowledging why I insisted he put a move on it. We were a nice distance from the resort, but he made up for it by speeding, but in a manner that felt somehow safe. It was obvious he knew these roads like the back of his own hand, and we were just shy of danger. He pressed down on the gas and it felt effortless, as if, before I could blink, we were in front of the resort.

As soon as he shifted the car in park, everyone hopped out. I was dreading the rest of this night more than he could imagine, and hopelessly wished I could remain and drive off with him. But I had to make sure that they didn't tear up anything, because I wasn't paying for a damn thing I didn't break.

The key didn't unlock the door fast enough before they were inside, picking up where they left off. Me and Lauren found ourselves taking front row seats to the rest of this telenovela.

Camille's jaw had started to swell from where Olivia's punches landed.

I was rather surprised, because I had not anticipated anything so severe.

"What the hell is wrong with you, Olivia?" Camille shouted. "Why would you just run up on me like that and attack me."

"Girl, go straight to hell, you home wrecking whore!" Olivia's voice cracked as she pointed her finger and yelled. Fresh tears fell again, leaving more traces of eye makeup smudged on her cheeks.

Camille mocked her. A scowl stretched across her lips.

"He doesn't want you. He never did," she announced. "It's about time you finally figured it out, though I'm not surprised it's taken you this long. You've always been ditzy as hell."

Lauren's eyes widened.

She turned and looked at me as she searched my face for answers. I had none. None that I planned to speak on. Staying out of this meant my knowledge of all this would remain quiet.

"All this time...all this time," Olivia mumbled. "All this time you knew, and you said nothing. How long?" she asked her. "How long have you been sleeping with my husband, Camille?"

Since your wedding, I thought, but I suppressed that comment with every bit of willpower, wishing and hoping against hope that it was not actually true.

"Shortly before you got married," Camille admitted boldly.

Olivia's jaw dropped. She was dumbfounded. So was I. I knew about *something-something* going down all those years ago, but Camille had looked me straight in my eye and told me a bold-faced lie.

Something clicked in Olivia's head, and she charged Camille again. This time she went full force, kick-boxing and slamming her down onto the hardwood floor, leaving Camille no time to brace herself. They fought on the floor until Lauren and I broke them up again.

"Camille, you are out of line!" I finally yelled.

"Screw you, Ava! You walk around here, pretending to be her friend, consoling her and acting surprised when you knew all along."

185

Olivia's neck did a three-sixty in my direction. I narrowed my eyes. Camille obviously wanted company on her side of karma. I sighed deeply, knowing I was going to have to explain what she meant.

"Liv, I—" I started to say, but she held up her hand to stop me.

"Save it. Better yet, don't say another thing to me in this life," she screamed. "I don't need any of you. Especially you..." She pointed at Camille. Olivia looked between us one last time then turned and stormed off.

21

Chapter Twenty One: Villains Play Victim Too

There was an uncanny silence throughout the villa. Sleep evaded me most of the night, as I laid in bed tossing and turning over what happened between Olivia and Camille. The guilt of not telling Olivia when I had the chance weighed heavily on me. It seemed I had failed both Lauren and Olivia in that area. When I thought I was protecting their feelings, I was actually doing them a disservice. Even though I wasn't the culprit, I was definitely still complicit in the wrongdoing.

Last night helped me see that quite clearly, after I saw the crushing disappointment on Olivia's face. She was already dealing with Desmond's betrayal, and then Camille's knife in her back, only to turn around and hear I had also omitted the truth. Lying by omission. Its a thing. I freed the burdensome breath that had my lungs in bondage. I flicked the tear forming in the corner of my eye into the air.

Closing my eyes, I did my breathing exercises to calm myself. I had no idea what the day was about to bring, but I knew there was going to be some difficulty, how could it not be a rough day? I rolled over to pick up my phone. I needed to talk to Jade badly. Even if she blames me, or has no kind words, at least I will hear a familiar friendly voice.

I considered waiting to tell her how left things went— give her the full scoop over cocktails— once I got back to LA, which could be any minute now. I was so ready to bail on this trip, but I also couldn't just take off without seeing Tate again.

Still, I needed a dose of her humor and wittiness to help me through the rest of this trip. I was five seconds away from packing my stuff and going home. The only thing saving me from another random anxiety attack was this private jet subscription plan, where I could literally call the concierge and go! Get out of dodge. With my anxiety, that was an essential service.

Unlocking my phone, I opened my favorites and tapped on her name. I rolled onto my back, and propped up on the pillows for a nice long chat, as the phone rang in my ear.

"Well hello, stranger," she answered, "Good to know you're still alive."

"Hey, cousin, what are you up to?"

"Getting ready for work. What are you up to?"

"Girl," I said. "Chilllleeee."

"Aww hell, what happened?"

"I don't even know where to start." I rubbed my hand over my forehead. "Jade, so much has happened, like Maury Povich, Jerry Springer level kind of stuff."

"Shut up!" she shouted dramatically. "Come on, spill it. I got fifteen minutes to spare."

I shook my head. She probably didn't have fifteen minutes, but she didn't care. Jade went to work whenever she 'got good and ready,' as she liked to say, and let it be known she could've easily called off whenever her boss said something.

"Jade," I said, pausing to gather my thoughts. "Olivia beat Camille's ass last night. And I don't mean *playground beat her ass*, I mean dragged her across the pavement, *MGM fight night* beat her ass!'"

"Whaaattttt!!" she screamed in surprise. "It's about time!"

She clapped loudly in my ear as she belted out a laugh. Jade was the only person I had ever told about Camille and Desmond since she wasn't in our friend group and I knew she could definitely keep a secret. Jade had a 100% solid track record of keeping my own secrets, and that's what cousins were born to do, right?

Jade had never been a fan of Camille's even prior to finding out about her treacherous ways. She always felt she was shady and entitled. No lies told there.

"Yes, girl. It was a hot ghetto mess and on camera too!" I laughed replaying the events in my mind. "I couldn't even break it up because I was stuck."

"Please, I would've let it happen on GP. That girl has had that beat down coming for a long time." Jade could not contain her giggles.

I nodded, silently agreeing with her.

"So it was that bad, huh?" Jade asked, once she gathered herself.

"Bad is an understatement. I didn't even know Olivia had it in her. It was like watching a Mike Tyson fight all over again. The way she pounced on Camille; Camille didn't stand a chance. My face was riddled with disbelief as she two-pieced her over-and-over."

Jade laughed infectiously in my ear.

I knew calling her would help me feel a little better. Jade took a few deep breaths before starting back up again.

"Please tell me you recorded it, please," she begged.

"Did you hear me when I said I was shocked into silence? Speechless! Girl, my mouth was open so wide, folks could see my tonsils."

"Damn! Now that scene, with Camille getting her due, well, I would've come to see."

I groaned. "Jade, I was so embarrassed."

"Why? You weren't fighting?! Ohmigosh, please tell me you weren't fighting, Ava. Because Aunty Vee will have an absolute fit if you get 'slandered online!'" Jade imitated my mother's caribbean accent, and the way she used 'slandered online' repeatedly to scare us all into *'respectable behavior befitting a Christian woman, proudly representing our island.'*

"No! Never! You know I get embarrassed easily. It's the second-hand embarrassment that's killing me," I told her, laughing at myself.

"Humph, not me. I don't get second-hand embarrassment, embarrassment adjacent, none of that. You act a damn fool, that's on you...not me."

I smiled. I imagined she was shrugging through the phone. Jade rambled on in my ear about all the reasons why she would've happily kept the crowd back so Olivia could handle her business. Jade was loyal to her core and despised people who weren't.

"I haven't even told you the worst part yet," I confessed.

"What, there's more?" she asked, curiously.

I sighed heavily. "Yeah, Camille threw me under the bus too. Told Olivia I knew all along and pretended not to know. Girl, I was outdone." I sighed, letting go of the worst of it and handing that bit over to my cousin to lay out the recovery plan, if one was even possible.

"So then you hopped up and beat her ass some more?" Her response was rhetorical, but I knew she was expecting some sort of response from me.

"I wanted to do just that, trust me, but I was too focused on Olivia's reaction that I didn't even bother responding to her." Besides, she knows I am a lover, not a fighter. I don't do fists, I don't do earring pulls, none of that. I will call an attorney and be done with it, in a heartbeat.

"Aw naw, see this is why I should've come because while you were focused on Olivia, I would've had Camille in a headlock. Y'all been letting her slide for too long with her slick-ass mouth. Her behavior should've been checked a long time ago."

She's right, I thought, staring at the ceiling.

I opened my mouth to respond when I suddenly heard yelling. Rolling my eyes, I sat up. I was in no way in the mood to deal with this today, but I knew round three was on the horizon. *One of them has to go.* I wasn't spending my last two days like this.

"Jade," I interrupted her, "I need to call you back. They've started back up again."

"Oh wow, girl, y'all are crazy. Let's get reeeaaaady to ruuummmm-ble," she shouted, mimicking Michael Buffer.

I burst out laughing. Jade was hilarious without even trying. We stayed in trouble because she was always cracking jokes when she shouldn't have been.

"Okay sis, bye!" I said.

"No, wait! Take your phone, press record," she instructed me. "Just in case another heavyweight fight is about to kick off. I need something to laugh at when you come home."

"Goodbye, Jade," I said with a smile in my voice, hanging up, but amused and thankful for my dear cousin being in my corner, no matter what life was throwing my way.

I climbed out of bed and headed down the hall. Peeking around the corner, I saw Camille pacing in the front room angrily as she held her phone close to her lips. The grip she had on it, I just knew she was going to launch it across the room at any moment.

"Des, this is the fifth time I've called you. Why the hell aren't you answering? I need to talk to you. Your little wife found out about us last night and it's time to tell her you're leaving her. You need to call me now!" Camille hung up the phone and tossed it on the couch.

I shook my head. She was seriously still trying to build a life with this man. A known cheater. Her naivety was at an all-time high right now. Gazing from behind the corner, I saw Lauren walk into the room.

Annoyance consumed her face as she stopped just shy of where Camille was pacing.

"I know I didn't just hear you say what I think I did," she snapped at Camille. "Are you seriously still chasing after a married man?"

I repositioned myself and leaned against the wall with my arms folded. I had plenty of words for her, but I'd let Lauren get hers out first. I was always the first one who called people to the carpet. She could have it this time. Besides, I wasn't confident I wouldn't slap the hell out of Camille just yet.

"Lauren, go worry about your own husband, and stay out of my business," Camille scoffed.

Oh crap. This is about to get ugly.

Lauren rolled her neck.

"And what the hell is that supposed to mean?"

Camille turned to face her.

"It means while you're worried about who I'm sleeping with, you should be focused on your own marriage. Out here giving marriage advice and you laid up with a cheater yourself."

I gasped. Camille's audacity knew no bounds.

Lauren scowled at her.

"At least I have a husband I can give advice about. What do you have, Camille? Other than a high body count and being somebody's side piece."

My jaw dropped even lower. Oh, she went *there*.

Camille balled up her fist.

"Please, by all means," she challenged her. "I'd be happy to pick up where Olivia left off."

I furrowed my brow. Speaking of which...where was Olivia?

Camille narrowed her eyes. Lauren didn't flinch.

"Lauren, I suggest you mind your business and stay out of mine," Camille reiterated.

An evil smirk formed across Lauren's lips. Camille got her snide comments off easily and often on Olivia, but we all knew Lauren was not Olivia, and she wouldn't back down as quickly. I stepped out from my hiding spot, deciding it was time to intervene before the second fight got started again.

"Where is Olivia?" I asked, putting the attention back where it should be. I couldn't care less about how Camille was feeling. "Is she here?"

Camille cut her eyes at me. And Lauren shifted hers towards me, shaking her head.

"No," Lauren answered. "She left a few hours ago. She and her film crew have left the building. I heard her on the phone with the airline after she cussed Desmond out repeatedly last night. She's gone."

My heart sank.

I truly wanted an opportunity to at least apologize before she left. This is not how I wanted things to end. She deserved to hear the truth. I owed her that much. Discovering your husband was a liar and a cheat was painful enough, but then to learn your friends were involved, through lies of omission, only magnified that hurt, to unimaginable levels. I could not fathom what she was going through, and hoped never to be in her shoes.

"Did she say anything before she left?" I asked Lauren.

"No," she replied sadly.

"Whatever," Camille blurted out.

Lauren snarled at Camille.

"I hope you get whatever you got coming," she said viciously.

Camille flashed a crooked smile. "I did her a favor," she boasted. "At least she knows who she's dealing with now. Desmond has always loved me. He just settled for Olivia. Just like you did for Trent."

Whoosh.

I pursed my lips at the same time my eyebrows touched my forehead. Camille never knew when to leave well enough alone. Lauren stepped into her face and pointed at her.

"You're going to watch your mouth about my marriage or else," she threatened.

"Or else what, Lauren?" Camille questioned. She glared at Lauren waiting for her reply. "I didn't think so. At least Olivia was bold enough to admit her marriage was a sham. You're still walking around here acting like yours is perfect when we all know better."

"You don't know anything at all about my life, honey, we *lost touch*, remember?" Lauren rebutted sarcastically.

I watched the exchange between them. Completely speechless. Camille rolled her eyes then smirked.

"We all know that it is a lie. Trent is the original cheater and probably still is."

I winced.

"Camille, that's hitting way below the belt," I intervened. "You're as wrong as two left shoes and you're standing here throwing shade at folks. What the hell is wrong with you?"

She turned her attention towards me.

"Ava, Ava, Ava..." she mocked, looking between me and Lauren. I knew she was about to stir the pot more than she already had. "By the way, did you ever tell Lauren the real reason why you didn't show up to her wedding."

I glared at Camille. Ready to carry out Lauren's threat. She grinned maliciously as she stared at Lauren. "Like I said, Lauren, worry about your own marriage."

"Why are you so worried about my marriage, Camille? Did you screw *my* husband too? Don't seem like that's beneath you these days."

Camille huffed arrogantly. "I date *real* athletes. Men with real potential. Nobody wants that has-been but you, honey. He's nothing more than some tired community...."

"Shut up Camille!" I interjected to stop this from getting any worse, going any lower.

Lauren wasn't packing any patience, not today. *No she didn't! What did she think Desmond was?* Lauren cocked her arm back and brought her hand to Camille's cheek—hard and loud— slapping her head to the side. It appeared she was no longer taking the high road.

"What the hell, Lauren!"

Lauren pointed at her again. "I said watch your mouth about my marriage and I meant it."

"This entire friend group is a joke!" Camille exclaimed. "You all are nothing to me, you are nothing more than a bunch of lies and fakeness. Violent!" Camille paused to point aggressively at Lauren, and she swung her finger in my direction before declaring "and *bitter* chicks that can't face reality. Let the past go! I'm out of here!"

"Good!" Lauren said, stepping aside as Camille rushed past her holding her cheek. We looked at each other as we watched Camille stomp out of the room like Olivia had the night before.

This was a disaster beyond belief. Nothing, absolutely nothing, had been *handled.*

22

Chapter Twenty Two: Magic Hour

The sunrise sat on top of the horizon like a beautiful blanket of pastel watercolors. It was the last one I would see from this magical place. Layers of red and orange shades were stacked on top of each other like puzzle pieces designed to fit each other perfectly. The waves lapped the shore and created the most serene, and desperately needed, calming rhythm.

"This is just beautiful, Ava," Lauren whispered as she stared in amazement. "You were right, just amazing."

I grinned, taking in all of the majestic scenery as we marveled at the glory in front of us. The birthday trip had gone to hell in a hand basket, but here we were, looking at a little slice of heaven.

No matter what, I felt so grateful to have had this time away. I had to give my type A self some credit for being willing just to unplug and make the effort to reconnect with my friends, even if it did not go perfectly.

God is good, all the time. I refused to let their dramas distract me from my morning ritual. I was still going to praise Him on my birthday vacay.

I grabbed Lauren's hand and closed my eyes, and began to speak out loud a short prayer of thanks, with a request for forgiveness for us all, collectively.

"Amen!" Lauren and I agreed on the need for peace and the need to turn this entire situation over to the Lord to work out.

I stopped short of praying for restoration, but that prayer might happen privately. I didn't want Lauren laughing in my face. I had no idea if I could imagine seeing any of them again, to be honest. I had hoped for a new beginning, a clean slate. Oh, well.

Lauren's flight home would leave in a few hours, and I wanted to share this moment with her. This trip had brought on a lot of things. Some good, plenty of bad, but clarity, nevertheless. I was clear about a lot of things.

About a lot of people.

I was happy that Lauren and I were at least able to mend our friendship. Saddened by the way Olivia and I parted. Relieved to be truly free of Camille's toxicity. Enamored by the sheer pleasure I felt to have become acquainted with Tate. Utterly elated that I turned the page in this new chapter.

Lauren nudged me.

"Everything's going to be okay with Olivia you know," she said, seeing the wheels turning in my head. "Give her some time and some space, then give her a call."

I smiled and nodded again.

"I know. I never wanted her to find out like this though," I admitted.

"Me either, but some things are out of our control."

Tell me about it. I leaned back on my hands. I could've predicted a ton of ways it would have come out, but not this. Anything but this.

"There's no perfect way to tell someone they're being betrayed," Lauren said, reading my thoughts. "Nor is there a perfect time or place to hear it."

I let go of the torment I was feeling and took in what she said. This was perfect advice. Lauren had always been whip smart, and able to solve problems that eluded most of us. I should have confided in her years ago, because she probably would have known how to handle it in a much smoother manner. Although she was right, it still stung. "I should've told her a long time ago. Same as you."

"Yeah, you should've, but what's done is done," Lauren advised.

I appreciated her honesty. It was the one thing we always shared. Regardless of how ugly it may have been, we had that. All the way up until her wedding.

She leaned back. "I hate that I came so late. This would've been nice to enjoy for a few days."

I tilted my head and nodded, silently agreeing with her as we gazed out into the horizon. I was going to miss this. But I was grateful that I had the experience.

"It was. Maybe we should plan another trip some time soon," I suggested.

"That'd be nice. Or I can come visit you in LA. I'm sure the sunrises are just as beautiful there."

They are. I smiled. "Sounds like a plan."

"What are you doing the rest of the day?" she inquired.

A smile formed on my lips. I turned to look at her, trying not to blush at the thought of him. "I'm going to be meeting up with Tate. He's planned this romantic day-date."

"Hmm, sounds like fun. Is he someone you would continue dating?"

My smile shifted, uneasy about attempting to even predict the future.

"What?" She looked at me. "Did I say something wrong?"

"No, it's just I live in LA, and he lives here."

"Okay, what's the problem? That's not even a four-hour flight between the two of you. And let's not act like you can't afford it, Ava."

I asked, "And what is that supposed to mean? Besides, Tate would be the one affording flights, ma'am, not me."

She chuckled lightly, then turned her body towards me.

"It means stop sabotaging something, in fear that it might plummet. I haven't seen you smile like that in a long time. You look exactly like how you looked when Sean asked you to be his girlfriend freshman year."

"Ugh! Don't bring him up." I playfully shoved her.

"What I'm saying is...I know how you look when you really like someone. Your eyes glisten, all thirty-two teeth are visible, and your entire disposition is different." She turned back around and sat back on her hands. "If he makes you happy, Ava, you owe it to yourself to see it through to the end. You deserve to be happy too."

I swallowed, with goal of thwarting the cry I felt inching up my throat.

"*You deserve happiness!*" Lauren was more emphatic this time. Her heartfelt words touched me more than she knew. They cut through the fear that had begun to build a wall between my heart and him.

"Thank you," I whispered.

She patted my hand, to confirm that we had touched and agreed on me finding love, at last. For perhaps the first time on this trip, I felt supported and surrounded by sincere friendship.

We sat in silence for a little while longer, taking in the stillness and beauty we were surrounded by. I fixated on the orange and yellow bright ball of sun that began to slowly appear, shifting the sky. Things had shifted, for sure. I felt new, refreshed.

The ocean was peaceful. I stared at the calm waves that brushed against the shoreline before slowly fading backwards, and then returning, with certainty.

"Time for me to head to the airport." Lauren dusted the sand off of her hands, then stood to her feet. "Need to get back home. I'm sure the kids are really missing me," she said, smiling.

I stood up to walk back with her.

"About what Camille said earlier," I recounted.

"Don't—" Lauren held up her hand. "Camille is the last person who gets to comment on my marriage after she ruined someone else's."

She had an excellent point. As of today, Camille needs to be officially canceled.

"I'm fully aware of the person I married. Whether I knew about him coming on to any of you all or not, I willingly walked into that situation, even knowing he had previously cheated on me. Am I happy about what was kept from me? No. But like I told you earlier, what's done is done. Trent and I aren't perfect, no marriage is. Olivia knows that and one day, maybe you will too. However, the life we've built together was worth fighting for. I really don't understand why folks insist on being in other folk's bedroom business?" Lauren stood resolute.

I gave her a bit of side-eye. I couldn't help it. I didn't appreciate that she wanted to lump me into their *'misery meets on mondays' club, that one day I would understand the imperfect marriage.* No, ma'am. I had high hopes for a happy and faithful marriage. I hated when people made excuses for cheaters. I could try to be less judgmental, but...

Lauren continued, "People grow from their mistakes, Ava." She seemed to be so tired, but also so passionate about this topic, it was weird to watch her try to rationalize. "Listen, Trent is not the same man I married all those years ago, fresh out of college. We have all changed, in so many ways. Girl, look at you- we have changed in the best possible way!" Lauren smiled. "So yes, I trust my husband. No matter what these girls say, I'm not going to turn my household upside down, and I am not going looking for anything either." Okay, well, then she knows where she stands, you have to give her that.

Lauren grabbed my hands.

"Ava, relationships are what you make of them. What the heck, just look at our girls, the fab four, from college until today? Some for the better, some for the worst. But you have to be open to that. Neither Trent, nor I, are the same people we were in college, or even the day that we said 'I Do', or when we had each child I've brought into this world. Every decade has revealed different things about us that we've grown to love. I know I used to be totally obsessed with perfection, but marriage and motherhood have taught me there's no such thing. No. Such. Thing. As. Perfect!" She kept getting louder and louder, as if we weren't just a few feet apart, and in the same room.

Finally, I decided to meet her in the middle: "True perfection is embracing the imperfections." I whispered it, and I embraced the words myself, and I wanted her to know that she was being heard, I appreciated her sharing, I got the message.

I stared at her teary-eyed, loving this sharing of wisdom and the open hearted vibe she was giving- after all of that petty drama, I needed this moment.

Looking at her, it was evident she was truly happy. I loved how in spite of everything, she'd evolved in her own way. I closed the gap and we hugged, with genuine affection. Nobody is perfect, we try our best, but we will never be. The key to love then is in the acceptance and in receiving the intention to love. All of us gathered here, with the intention to love, and that was what ultimately mattered. This was the clarity about the past, and the reconnection I was searching for, and I found it.

23

Chapter Twenty Three: CPR

T*wo months later*

I sat in a booth on the patio at the Nordstrom cafe, having a Chai latte and french onion soup. The warmth of the afternoon sunshine felt amazing on my skin, as I had already started to miss the laying about in the sun at the villa in Cabo. Not to mention how I missed Tate. I was glad to have the chance, at last, to meet up with Olivia, but I also could not wait to get back into Tate's arms.

I was still hoping that she showed up. I hated the way things ended between Olivia and me, and I wanted to fix it. What I did, although not as bad as Camille, was still horrible. I withheld information thinking I was remaining neutral when in fact I had chosen a side. I just didn't realize it then of course, but I was being unfair, when I thought I was just doing what was best for everyone involved at the time.

Once I returned, Jade helped me see the error of my ways.

I spilled every single detail about the birthday and so-called reunion trip, and once I finished, she held that accountability mirror up to my face. I'd been so focused on remaining neutral, maintaining my loyalty to both of my best friends, when in fact not telling Olivia was absolutely me betraying her. Perhaps, seeing it from that perspective pushed me to delve deep into making amends with her.

I owed her a sincere, genuine apology. None of that, *"if you feel I hurt you"* type of dodging the issue, but a heartfelt one that takes actual accountability. I really hoped that we could move past this.

Sipping my latte, I stared at the door. We were supposed to be meeting at 1:30 p.m. and it was already five minutes until two. I was getting antsy about her flaking on me. It took close to six emails, with me being extremely persistent, sweetly persuasive, before she finally agreed to meet. Of course, this was my wheelhouse, persuading people to do things. But at least I was using it for good. Sitting here, I couldn't help but think she was going to pull another Cabo stunt, except this time she wouldn't show at all.

I retrieved my phone from my purse. My ringer had been switched to vibrate to give us the privacy and attention this conversation warranted. I initially invited her to my place for dinner, so that we could speak undisturbed and freely. She nixed that idea and told me she'd rather meet for lunch in public, on neutral ground.

At first I was against meeting out, concerned about the embarrassing truths being revealed. The last thing I wanted was another *Olivia v. Camille* confrontation. Besides, I fundamentally did not believe private issues should be discussed in public, based on my upbringing in the church and also, the teachings of Vera Richards: *'you will act like a lady at all times!'*

No missed calls.

I turned my lip up and slid the phone back into my handbag. I would give her ten more minutes and then I would leave. Even if I were the one in the wrong, I certainly wasn't going to sit here like an idiot.

The metal wind chimes over the door clinked against one another, pulling my focus from my thoughts back to the entrance. When I looked across the cafe, I finally saw Olivia looking around for me. I raised my hand and waved it for her to see where I was seated. She nodded acknowledging she saw me and pointed to the counter to let me know she was going to grab something first.

I straightened in my chair then said a small prayer that this went smoothly. I lifted my cup to sip and prepare my throat for a long chat. *You got this, Ava,* I chanted to myself, shaking off the nervousness that swept over me. Olivia wasn't usually an unhinged person, but that was pre-Desmond cheating. Post Desmond cheating could be different altogether. Her heavyweight bout in Cabo was evidence of that.

Olivia strolled towards me.

"Hey," I said, standing up to hug her.

She placed her cup down and hugged me back.

"Hey," she said, sitting down.

Relief passed over me to see she was at least open to starting this off right. Jade had warned me to be ready for anything—good or bad. *'Prepare for the worst, but expect the best,'* was more along the lines of what she said.

"Thank you for coming," I jumped right out and told her. "I appreciate you taking this meeting."

She nodded as she sipped her drink.

"Olivia, I want to begin by apologizing to you. Upon my return, I did some serious self-reflecting. It took Jade showing me a different perspective, and I have realized that yes, I had chosen a side even when I was trying not to, for everyone's sake. I was wrong for my part in Camille's deception and I'm sorry. I should've told you the second that I found out. I guess I was torn between being loyal to you or betraying her. And I didn't want to choose sides. I loved you both equally. I'm not making any excuses; I only want you to see where I was coming from and why I did what I did. It wasn't until I saw that look in your eyes that I knew for sure that I'd made the wrong decision."

She gave me a half-smile, obviously not convinced.

I continued, "Truth is, that's the reason why Camille and I fell out. I told her that she needed to tell you or I would. We got into a huge fight, and she stopped talking to me."

Her eyes widened.

"Ava, when I asked you why you weren't talking to her, you brushed me off," she scolded. "Another lie."

I shook my head.

"I know and I'm sorry for that too."

Olivia had known why Lauren and I fell out, but I never confided in her about the dissolution of my friendship with Camille because I wasn't ready to tell her the truth. Same as Lauren, I was afraid she'd get upset and stop talking to me altogether. History had proven women tended to react weirdly after they found out their significant other was cheating. I was trying to avoid that on the off-chance Camille did the right thing.

But as the years passed, and the distance grew between us, time brought about a certain amount of clarity. Although I wasn't thrilled about her betrayal, we had history just like I did with Olivia.

"Why didn't you just tell me the truth?" she questioned.

"Honestly Liv, I didn't feel like it was my place. I threatened Camille hoping she would either confess or stop. Plus, I'd gone through that with Lauren already and we see how that turned out. I figured your relationship was your business. I always knew karma would eventually bite Camille in the ass."

She stared at me sternly.

"You should've told *me*," she repeated. "You could've saved me the embarrassment of finding out like I did, when I did."

I nodded knowingly.

"You're right."

"Since we're being transparent, when did you find out?" she queried. "How long has it been going on?"

I furrowed my brow.

This was not a question I wanted to answer, but she was right. I sold this meeting under the guise we could be transparent and speak freely, so I had to be forthcoming.

"Olivia..."

"No, Ava. You said nothing was off limits, so tell me. Right now. How long was my supposed best friend having an affair with my soon-to-be ex-husband?"

She picked up her cup and sipped. Waiting for me to tell her what I dreaded confessing.

"Before you got married."

Her eyes opened wider causing the wrinkle in her forehead to deepen. I thought she was about to spit out her tea, because I certainly would have. Her jaw dropped and her eyebrows went sky high.

"Excuse me?"

I nodded shamefully. I hated having to do this.

"Desmond said they started sleeping together two years ago—after our housewarming party."

Desmond definitely lied. I gave her a confused look. Then I shook my head to let her know that wasn't the truth.

"No, they may have picked back up then, but they definitely slept together before your wedding. I'm not sure how long before then, but that's where my knowledge of them starts."

She released an exasperated breath.

"I have to be honest, Ava. Finding out you knew and didn't say anything, even after the outburst at the pool party, that really hurts. You knew why she was tripping with me the whole time and kept quiet. I couldn't for the life of me figure out where her animosity for me stemmed from, then after everything came out, it made sense. On the flight home I had time to replay everything. All the way back to when we first walked in on her in the kitchen on the phone. She was talking to Des, and I had no clue. But you did," she pointed out.

"Liv, I didn't know she was talking to him. I swear I didn't."

"But you suspected," she stated. "Look me in my eye and tell me you didn't."

I sighed.

"At that point, no I didn't." It was the truth. At that exact moment, I hadn't. But after that first dinner together, my suspicions grew.

"Okay, what about any time during the trip?"

Damn.

"Yes. Once you blurted out you suspected he was cheating at the first dinner we had, I wondered if it could be the worst case scenario, and so I confronted her. I asked if she was still sleeping with him. She denied it so I left it alone."

The words burned leaving my lips. They seemed a lot worse saying them now than before.

Olivia smirked. And I wasn't sure if she was pissed or over it. I stretched my arm across the table and placed my palm on top of her hand.

"I don't know if you can ever forgive me, but I hope you can. My intentions were purely genuine. I didn't want to hurt either of you. Liv, I really enjoyed the time we spent in Cabo, minus the drama. I want us to repair our friendship and move forward. I miss you, Liv."

Crippling silence filled the space between us. She mulled over my words. My eyes remained on her as I waited for her answer. Her body sat rigid in her chair while keeping me on the edge of mine. A few seconds later, she leaned forward and placed her free hand on top of mine.

"I will agree to forgiving you and us repairing our friendship on one condition," she commanded.

"Anything, you name it," I willingly complied.

"Don't ever lie to me again, Ava. I don't care if you think it will rip me to shreds; I want the truth. Let me deal with processing it how I see fit. But you, you tell me the truth. Otherwise, I don't want to be friends."

I scooted my chair back, stood up and walked over to her. Bending over, I hugged her tightly.

"Deal."

Epilogue: Forever, For Always, For Love

"You look beautiful," Tate said, glancing over at me. "That dress has several naughty thoughts going through my mind."

I blushed.

"Thank you," I said, then blew him an air kiss.

He nibbled on his bottom lip, and I imagined the thought that was racing through his mind at this exact moment. His eyes trailed over my body, stopping at my exposed thigh, and back up to my eyes. The salacious smile on his face sent electrified shock waves through my body, in the best possible way.

"A penny for your thoughts?" I asked coyly.

"Oh, you don't want to know what I'm thinking right now," he answered seductively. "Because if I told you, I'd have no choice but to act on these thoughts, and we have to get to the opening."

"Oh yeah?" I murmured.

"Yes."

I arched my eyebrow sinfully. Curious to see just how far he'd take this. I winked at him then slowly traced my tongue across my lips. A silent acceptance of his challenge. He grinned at me. I crossed my leg to expose more of my thigh through the high split. The emerald-green material popped against my chestnut complexion.

He shook his head. Attempting to rid himself of the naughty thoughts running amuck through out his mind. I felt beautiful. Sexy. But beneath

Tate's gaze, I felt like a celestial being. His queen to be worshiped and revered.

I *loved* this man. I loved how he loved me back.

There was no question about it. This past year has felt like a dream come true. After our date in Cabo where we sailed on a yacht—talking, dancing, and laughing—he asked if we could continue dating past the week and a half we spent there. I was reluctant at first. I'd never believed in a having long-distance relationships. Honestly, relationships were hard enough without adding complications to it, logistics of travel and the constant longing for someone that couldn't be there for you. Not being able to see him regularly didn't seem like something I wanted to commit to, as a measure of self-preservation.

Then I remembered what Lauren said. And she was right. I deserved happiness too. I owed it to *myself* to see this through to the end.

Turns out, Tate resided in Los Angeles and stayed only in Cabo for three months to train and oversee a new head chef for his restaurant. And even better than that, he lived on the west side! Just living in Los Angeles could have still landed us in a long distance relationship, but thankfully he was west of the 405, and so for him, it was just a short drive to see me. Our frequent dates were easy and effortless, and our bond seemed to grow stronger every day.

Tate lifted my hand to his lips and kissed it.

"I appreciate you sharing your birthday with my grand opening. I know you wanted to go to Paris, but I promise I'll make it up to you."

I smiled at him.

"There's no other way I would rather spend my birthday than celebrating with you," I replied. "This is a big night for you."

He placed another kiss on my hand.

It was true. I was ecstatic to celebrate his latest business endeavor. Rhythm and Roots Kitchen was his fifth restaurant and his first in LA, which was a complete surprise to me. I would've thought with him living here, he'd already have a restaurant. But he explained how LA was flooded with restaurants, and the real estate market made it too risky and expensive, which I could cosign. Besides, he wanted to wait until he came up with the perfect idea, tried-and-true menu items and of course, the name for his restaurant launch.

"Did I ever tell you how much I love the name you chose?" I teased. The restaurant theme would be elevated soul food, classic southern dishes with a California flair. At last week's soft launch tasting, I was frankly blown away by the deliciousness of it all.

Tate cooked dinners for me all the time, but he had obviously held things back to surprise me. My favorite new dish was his innovative soul sushi, which looked like a regular sushi roll topped with spicy sauce, avocado and ginger, but in fact Tate made his version with collard greens, braised turkey thighs, and mac and cheese (the best I've ever tasted, by the way,) all encapsulated with a shell of seasoned brown rice. Emphasis on the *seasoned*. The brown rice alone had me craving more, but the entire dish together, baaaby, *whoa!*

He winked at me.

"You should, you inspired it. I love how you are so grounded, Ava. That's the roots. And then how we just flow so effortlessly when we are together, that's the rhythm." Tate glanced at me to see if I was receiving all of his emotional expression.

"I hope that you know, you are a big part of my success with this restaurant."

And I did know, but I liked hearing him say it. For the last few weeks, I had been giving a lot of marketing tips and offering up my best PR tactics to ensure he had a smooth launch. Normally I wouldn't want my boyfriend as a client, but Tate was different.

Over the weeks, I had made quite a few exceptions for Tate— working late into the evening on his PR strategy, giving him deep discounts on media buys— but one boundary had been upheld, and we were both proud of our self-restraint. It was not easy. At all.

Tate pulled onto the lot of his newest restaurant and my eyes gleamed with excitement. The exterior was a beautiful shade of deep teal, one of my favorite colors, with large paned windows encased by black iron. Two black awnings sat atop the windows and one over the entryway, very modern and chic. Sculptural plants and shrubbery flanked the stone columns in front. An incredible hand-painted mural along the wall highlighted the creativity and the uniqueness of Tate's establishment. I was highly impressed and I hadn't even gone inside.

"Are you ready?" he asked, trying to mask his excitement.

"Yes, I'm so ready, darling."

He opened his door, and I unbuckled my seat belt as he walked around to my side. He opened my door and helped me out, gazing at me like I was on the menu.

"Lord have mercy," he uttered.

My cheeks crimsoned at his admiration and also his old school vibe. Who even says, "Lord have mercy" anymore? But I loved hearing it roll off his lips.

"Ava Richards, you sure know how to make a man feel good about himself."

I playfully tapped his chest.

"Stop it, Tate, you're making me blush."

"Let's hope I can keep you blushing all night." He winked and held out his arm for me. I graciously slid mine through and cuffed his arm. "Are you ready, my beautiful lady?"

"Lead the way, my handsome king."

We walked up the cobblestone walkway to the door. He opened the door and I walked in.

"Surprise!" Everyone yelled at a level ten volume. Wow!

"Oh my God!" I shouted, looking around at all the people that were here. Friends, family, my colleagues. "What, I can't believe..."

"Happy birthday, baby," Tate whispered from behind me.

I turned to face him and saw the biggest smile plastered on his lips. He tricked me! And I never suspected a thing. I smiled the biggest cheese-ball smile at him, then turned back around to see everyone who came out. Here I was thinking he'd been spending weeks planning his grand opening to be perfection, and it was actually a surprise birthday party for me.

"Happy birthday, cousin," Jade said, hugging me with lots of warmth and excitement.

"You knew, didn't you?" I eyed her suspiciously.

"Of course I knew. Who do you think helped keep you occupied while he shopped and planned this beautiful party?" She grinned, very proud of the fact they were able to pull this surprise event off. "Did you suspect anything?"

I shook my head no, and I had not.

"You came too close once, but I switched up my approach and it was smooth sailing from there." Jade was so pleased that this was happening. She adored Tate like I did.

I chuckled. "Well I'm *so happy* that you're happy that you and my man pulled the wool over my eyes."

Jade shrugged off my perky sarcasm.

"*You're welcome*," she said, walking around me to hug Tate hello.

"Ava darling, happy birthday. You look fabulous," my mother complimented. "This dress is very flattering."

Having a compliment from Tate was special, but hearing it from my mother, well, I beamed. My sister always said: if Vera approves of an outfit, note that day in your journal.

I kissed her on her cheeks. "Thank you, Mother." I was so happy that she was here. Tate really did think of everything.

"Happy birthday, friend!" Lauren exclaimed loudly. "Hello, Ms. Vera."

"Lauren." My mother gave her a slight nod and walked off to speak to the other guests.

"Yes, happy birthday!" Olivia shouted from behind. "I can't believe it's been a year already. Oh my goodness! Remember this time last year we were in Cabo!"

"Who are you telling?" I giggled. "I swear I was just getting used to saying forty. Now I have to say forty-one."

We shared a long laugh. Since we reunited last year, we had been in almost constant contact. As much as we could with our busy lives, but we were all making a solid effort. Lauren had visited several times and was even considering relocating Trent and the kids to LA, and she would teach here at USC. I was all for it, because the only time I planned on heading east was during the warmer months.

Olivia's reality show was unfortunately canceled, despite our best efforts to turn up for the cameras in Cabo. The good news, I guess, is that she managed to land another television deal, without Desmond of course. She really has been doing great since her divorce, like, she was glowing from inside and she truly looked happier than ever.

"Let me go speak to the other guests, I'll be right back," I told them. The room was filled to capacity with folks. The reunion with familiar faces and the introduction to new ones enveloped me in that sense of belonging that I had been searching for all through my 30's, only to land here happily on my 41st birthday.

"Um, Ava, baby, hold up," Tate wrapped his arm around my shoulder and pulled me closer in to his chest.

"Babe, I'm just going to speak to everyone really quickly, thank them for coming," I informed him. I really wanted my etiquette to be on point, with so many coming from far and away to celebrate my special day again. I wanted to express my gratitude. Since last year's birthday trip, I really embraced the idea of showing my appreciation when I had the chance and making solid decisions with the people who matter in life.

"I know, but I just need a quick second." He was insistent that I stay close.

I gave him a peculiar look. A parade of waiters with trays began walking around, passing out glasses of champagne. Tate stood in front of me, waiting for everyone to receive theirs. Once everyone had a glass, the guests turned their attention to him.

"Ava," he started speaking in an even deeper pitch and louder tone, addressing everyone in the room, all while laser-focusing on me.

I smiled at the sound of my name leaving his lips.

"This past year has been the best year of my life. I never imagined I would meet the true love of my life on a work trip, but I did, and here we are. Being with you has opened my perspective to a whole new world. I've traveled around the world many times over, yet I found a home in you. I've never met a woman like you. Ambitious. Driven. Intelligent. You're a breath of fresh air..."

Tate handed his glass to Jade then reached into his pocket, pulling out a robin's egg blue-colored box. Lauren nudged me repeatedly with her elbow. I bumped her back with mine, to urge her to stop. I was trying hard enough to keep it together, I could feel tears welling up.

He continued. "While planning this event, I thought long and hard about what I wanted to say, how I wanted this to play out, and I decided to look up numbers and the meaning behind them. For those who don't know, Ava and I have spent many hours talking about God, our faith and a range of spiritually enlightening things during this journey together. And I researched two numbers...four and one. The age my beautiful woman has turned today."

I was crushing hard over him. The emotions I felt were evident of that. My heart pounded against my chest. My body was warm and pulsating. This was the opposite of those dreaded panic attacks, this was a *pleasure attack*.

Bated breaths seeped from my lips. I glowed from within. This man touched every part of me and without even placing a single finger on my body, I could feel his passion.

"According to my research, the number four means creation. It represents stability, order and is perceived to be a perfect number. It represents the elements and is a feminine number. While the number 1 signifies bringing your dreams into reality, a fresh start, a new beginning and the physical manifestation of your desires. Baby, this past year I have watched you dream, wish, grow, and bloom into this amazing woman, and I am privileged to have been afforded the opportunity to do so."

I felt the moisture glaze over my eyes. Tate walked over and knelt down in front of me. At that moment, Lauren took my champagne glass from me, and I placed my hand inside of Tate's.

"If life with you is anything like this past year, I want more of it." He opened the box to display a stunning oval-cut diamond set in a platinum band with diamonds. The ring was brilliant. Bold and bright, dazzling and feminine. Wow, it was just my style.

"Ava, would you do me the greatest honor and become my wife?"

I looked at him with tears in my eyes and a heartfelt smile on my lips. I beamed inside as I nodded at his proposal. "Yes, Tate. I will marry you."

As the words escaped Tate's lips, a wave of emotions washed over me, blending into a beautiful rhythm of joy, gratitude, and love. In that moment, surrounded by the warmth of our shared journey, I knew without a doubt that this was the beginning of a new chapter—one filled with endless possibilities and boundless love.

The last year had been a journey, reuniting with my girls, finding my own peace and settling into, ahem, middle age joy. And I wouldn't change a thing.

As Tate slipped the ring onto my finger, it sparkled under the restaurant's glittering lights—a tangible symbol of our commitment to each other. With tears of happiness glistening in our eyes, we embraced, feeling the weight of the past lifting off our shoulders, making room for a future together, bright with promise.

And as we stood there, locked in each other's arms, surrounded by the people in this world that we cared about the most, I whispered softly, "I can't wait to spend forever with you, Tate."

He whispered back, with a genuine and tender smile, "Forever sounds perfect, Ava."

About the Author

Zina Patel is the creative force behind gripping thrillers and heartwarming women's fiction. Based in Los Angeles, she crafts stories that blend suspense with depth, drawing inspiration from the city's energy, with its vibrant streets and diverse characters. Join Zina on an exhilarating journey through her captivating tales set by the Pacific Ocean, in her debut novel *Playa Vista Social Club* and her latest novel, *Wish You Had Told Me*.

THANK YOU FOR READING!

You can connect with me on:

🌐 http://www.zinapatel.com
📘 http://www.instagram.com/zinapatelbooks

Also by Zina Patel

Interested in Suspense Thrillers?

 Playa Vista Social Club delivers a page-turner tale of an idyllic Southern California neighborhood suddenly turned upside down by the disappearance of a popular social media star. Looking for a suspenseful tale of friendship, deception and the extreme measures people will take to protect their secrets?

Look no further- nonstop action and unexpected twists will keep you guessing until the very end. *Each neighbor has a story. One of them knows the truth.*

Available in paperback and Kindle on **Amazon**.

Love audiobooks? **Listen now on Audible or Spotify!**

Made in the USA
Monee, IL
12 June 2025

19321409R00135